I0788137

Dolphin Mimicry

Dolphin Mimicry

A story of a dolphin and a man
and their enlightened journey of personal discovery
in the South Atlantic off the coast of Namibia.

Roger James Kuhns

Leaning Rock Press, LLC
Gales Ferry, CT 06335
www.leaningrockpress.com
leaningrockpress@gmail.com

www.rogerjameskuhns.com
Cover Design by Roger Kuhns
Author Photo by Julia Minchew

978-1-950323-40-1, Hardcover
978-1-950323-41-8, Softcover
978-1-950323-42-5, eBook

Library of Congress Control Number: 2020924793

Publisher's Cataloging-In-Publication Data
(Prepared by The Donohue Group, Inc.)

Names: Kuhns, Roger James, author.
Title: Dolphin mimicry : a story of a dolphin and a man and their
    enlightened journey of personal discovery in the South Atlantic off the
    coast of Namibia / Roger James Kuhns.
Description: Second edition. | Gales Ferry, CT : Leaning Rock Press, [2021]
Identifiers: ISBN 9781950323401 (hardcover) | ISBN 9781950323418
    (softcover) | ISBN 9781950323425 (ebook)
Subjects: LCSH: Scuba divers--South Atlantic Ocean--Fiction. | Dolphins--
    South Atlantic Ocean--Fiction. | Human-animal relationships--Fiction.
Classification: LCC PS3611.U398 D65 2021 (print) | LCC PS3611.U398
    (ebook) | DDC 813/.6--dc23

Printed and bound in the United States of America, second edition

This story began as a bedtime tale for my children, Matthew and Madeleine, following my experiences at sea off the southwestern coast of South Africa and Namibia. I wrote the story while at sea exploring for diamonds, where I could see all the semi rigs drilling for oil on the continental shelf. During this time, I was lucky enough to watch dolphins, whales, sharks, and humans interacting in many ways.

So it is to
Matthew and Madeleine
I dedicate this book.

Reviews

"This is a story of joy and wonder. Kuhns is a superb writer, deftly teaching us the wonders of the ocean and marine life, woven into a remarkable story. If you pick up this book, cancel your plans - you will not be able to put it down."

Bill Young, Point Pleasant, NJ

"*Dolphin Mimicry* serves as a good reminder to us all about the beautiful, though complicated, relationship between animals and humans. I have to say the last few chapters had my heart racing. Overall a great read. If you respect our natural environment, can accept human fault, and believe in the power and wisdom of nonhuman beings, this novel is for you."

Alyssa Auvinen, Gresham, OR

"There were parts of the book where I was emotionally touched. I really liked how Jonas bonded with the dolphin, and how the dolphins have this love and protection for humans. I love the book."

Ron Brandes, Waterbury, CT

"This is a tale of an unusual friendship formed between man and dolphin, Jonas and Peek. It isn't just the lively and interesting characters or relationships that capture the reader's attention, it is the many facts riddled throughout. This book is well written, intelligent, intriguing, and it brings the reader on a journey of discovery, friendship, heartbreak, and the many wonders of the creatures of the waters. Sometimes to make a big change, we need to feel the awe and the wonder of something much, much larger than we are."

Rebecca Walsch, Mystic, CT

"Oh, my goodness, I'm in tears. I just finished *Dolphin Mimicry*. What a great ending, sad, but happy at the same time. Love it."

Robin Nelson, Gales Ferry, CT

Also by Roger James Kuhns

Didn't See That Coming

The Last Move

Navigating the Energy Maze with G. Shaw

ESCARPMENT, a film documentary

Evening with Jens Jensen, a performance film

Contents

Dolphin Mimicry

CHAPTER

1

Who knows the road to the sky?
Namibian proverb

Peek considered the feeling euphoric. Water surged around him as he pumped furiously to add extra push to his speed. The bow wave crashed and danced just above him, and the bubbles that formed in his wake were like a marine contrail. Peek shot out of the water and sucked in a breath of air before diving back into the bow wave.

Suddenly the pressure behind him subsided as the boat of man slowed down. Gracefully pumping his strong flukes, he swam to port, angling away from the boat and the man-made floating island in the water just ahead. He had grown used to the large, metal island, as he had grown used to the free rides on the bow waves of incoming and outgoing boats. It was a diversion, for now, for *these* humans were new to this part of the coast. Not like the ones he remembered from his youth. Because of those ancient memories, Peek was careful to investigate the new arrivals in his waters. But slowly he found that they were not like the humans he had known many years earlier. These had other tasks to do and were apparently not interested in him or his family. Except for the one human—that one was different.

Peek leaped from the water, high and proud, and eyed the scene. There was *the* human on the metal island, far above the water, looking at him. He had seen this human there before, and Peek again leaped from the water with all his strength and spiraled back into the ocean swell. At the height of his jump the world spun delightfully around, and within the pirouette the human seemed to spin also. In that instant of fluid primeval motion, as their eyes locked, Peek's thoughts seemed to blend momentarily with the human's.

Jonas Jeremy James, the man with three first names, was certain the dolphin had been watching him. It had jumped and spiraled in the air; its balletic motion was necromantic.

Most of the dolphins along the coast were distinctive because of their dark blue-black color above with light gray around the head and underside—they were Heaviside's dolphins. But this one was different, and Jonas thought it wasn't native to the area. Offsetting its dark satin gray color was a patch of white on its forehead, with white under its chin and chest and a stripe near its tail. Jonas noticed another distinctive white marking, perhaps a scar, that ran along the right side of its head. The unusual dolphin was easy to identify and seemed to mingle with the local shoal just fine. Jonas could usually spot the location of a shoal of dolphins, since the gulls typically flocked above them hoping for the leftovers from the dolphins' meal of fish. As it watched him, the dolphin at once gave him the sensation of being an alien, as well as an object of curiosity.

An alien? Man did not really belong in the sea, he was learning that now. Jonas's thirty-eighth birthday had been two days ago, and it had also marked the anniversary of twenty-one years at sea. During all those voyages and jobs he had gained an understanding of the ocean that few men had ever achieved. It was inherent in Jonas. It was in that knowledge that he knew man was out of his element here. It seemed evolution had purposefully forced the progenitors of his species away from the sea, but some distant memory drew people like Jonas back to the water. As for being an object of curiosity, why else would the dolphin watch him? Was this just his fanciful imagination? Jonas knew about dolphins, he knew they were smart. He had watched them at sea his whole life and had even swam with them on occasion. But what he was destined to learn about them in the coming months would change his life forever.

Jonas stood at the rail and looked out over the expanse of the steel-gray ocean. He came to this high spot on the drilling platform every afternoon for a coffee break. The black, bitter-sweet brew warmed him as he drank from a mug cupped in his large hands. Jonas was a big man, over six feet tall, and possessed a wiry strength from his diving career. He ran a hand through his close-cropped black hair. He had kind eyes, punctuated with crow's-feet from his easy smile and laughter.

Now he watched as a supply boat pulled up to its moorings alongside the lower level of the *Atlantic Stroom*, the semi-submersible drilling platform that was his home. Mariners called these things "floaters" or "semis" because they floated on huge pontoons submersed below the water. Other drilling platforms deployed in shallow water sat on long-legged foundations set in the seafloor. Those were called "standups." The semis were more versatile and could be moved more easily. But the *Atlantic Stroom* had been moored over an oil well off the Namibian coast for nearly eight months now. Jonas, so in tune with the sea, had long since become familiar with the local cetacean population.

One of the crew from the tender tossed a thick orange rope over to one of the *Atlantic Stroom*'s workers. The supplies would be off-loaded, and garbage on-loaded within an hour. The *Atlantic Stroom* acted as its own small floating town. It housed all the services and supplies needed to keep the marine town afloat, fed, and productive. The semi-submersible, as a 30,000-ton vessel, had its own azimuth thrusters to keep the rig positioned for its oil drilling and production operations. It rested on two massive submerged pontoons, attached to the above-water decks by six massive tubular steel legs. The crew of 150 people had all manner of tasks, from the captain to the engineers and mechanics, a doctor, drillers and helpers, cleaning staff, and scientists. Also on board were recreation and entertainment areas, living quarters, laboratories, maintenance shops, warehouses, laundry facilities, and of course the cafeteria.

The dolphin that had been riding the tender's bow wave became bored as the boat slowed and the wave diminished. It soon vanished into its aqueous world.

Topside, the wind had the bite of a southeaster blowing in from the Cape. It chilled to the bone any body exposed to the moist air on deck. There was a Roaring Forties cyclonic storm spiraling out of the cold waters to the south, where the Atlantic and Indian Oceans met. Jonas could tell this just by watching the long, three-meter-high swells that rolled under the *Atlantic Stroom*. Thin gray clouds masked enough sunlight to blanket the scene in even shades of gray.

A loud clang from the drill works shook Jonas's mind out of his daydreaming. He refocused on the man-made environment on which he stood. Life on a semi was noisy, a vibrating, thrumming world of activity. The constant hum of a half dozen different motors was the backdrop to harsher metallic clangs and resonating thuds from heavy equipment and drill steel banging against one another, orchestrated with the whine of cables running through winches and block and tackle arrays. Vibrations could also be felt, but not heard, like some strange heartbeat through the metal bulkheads and railings. Within the platform's working space, the noise drowned out the sound of the sea. It was only when standing on the exposed upper decks, or during massive storms, that the sea could be heard and felt. Jonas loved the sea more than the land—as do all good sailors—because while on it he was a mote in a limitless fluid world. He did not stand out, and that suited him.

CHAPTER

2

What eats you will not jump over you.
Namibian proverb

Jonas absently glanced at his watch and said to himself, "Well, well, well, down into the black hole." He had some diving to do before his shift was up. Tomorrow would also be a prolonged dive to strengthen one of the pontoon legs that formed the floating foundation of the platform. The leg had been damaged in the last storm several days ago. He turned and grabbed the rail of the steep metal stairs and climbed them two at a time up to the *Atlantic Stroom's* weather station.

The tall, slender Namibian who sat behind the television monitor was Bebe February. His skin was black as coal, not a hair on his head, and he possessed enormous hands that amazed Jonas, as the man seemed to operate a multitude of delicate controls.

Bebe February was a Kaokovelder, a gentle man from the desert and savanna tribes of Namibia, born among the dunes of the wind-sculpted Kaokoveld Desert. He had told Jonas that the sea was the other side of the desert, the antipode, both born of waves driven by wind and always in motion. Bebe said you could die of thirst and heat on the waves of one or drown and freeze to death on the waves of the other. He said it was God's odd humor that put them side by side, and God's greater humor that he drove men to live on both. Jonas recalled what Bebe had told him, *that the ocean and the desert do not get along, just as men of different villages do not get along. Just as the sand is spit from the sea back*

5

up onto the land, so is one stranger turned away from the village. But when Jonas said that the sea often took the sand, Bebe frowned at him. He had asked Bebe if that wasn't akin to one accepting the other? Bebe had said no, that it was just another example of theft, and that too was like man. Man, explained Bebe to Jonas, always asked for a little more when given a gift, and if not given more will take it in the name of some obscure justification.

Bebe had good reasons for such beliefs. He had worked in the coastal diamond fields—the Sperrgebiet—the so-called Prohibited Area. Cartographers labeled it the Skeleton Coast after the innumerable shipwrecks. But the Namibian laborers simply called it the Forbidden Lands. It was a diamond-rich 320-kilometer stretch of coast in Namibia and South Africa. Bebe and his father had worked more like slaves than employees under cruel conditions for virtually no pay.

Bebe and Jonas were veteran crew on the *Atlantic Stroom*, having served for five years together. They were, despite their vastly different upbringing and considerably different experiences in life, also very good friends.

"How's it look?" Jonas asked.

"Not too good, Jonas, not too good." Bebe February tapped the screen with his long, leathery black finger as he commented on the day's weather outlook, his fingernail clicking on the glass. "You see here that big nasty thing, that is another bad storm. Be here soon. You bet. After all, this is the stormy season." The big man shook his head, almost as if in sorrow, as his deep voice seemed to reverberate through the room.

The last storm had been a bad one that had rattled the crew's bones as well as the semi's steel skeleton. Jonas sensed that Bebe February was in no mood to reexperience such an event so soon. "When will she hit us? A couple days?" Jonas asked.

"Sooner. You bet." Bebe tapped the screen again. "Cape Town says this one has eighty-knot winds. Force 9. It'll be here in the morning at the earliest, dead right."

"Force 9," Jonas repeated in a harsh whisper. "Hmm, that's bad news. I haven't finished the welds on the starboard pontoon." The pontoon was more than a hundred meters long and twenty meters underwater and had been torqued and damaged in the previous storm. Jonas had yet to complete welding repairs on its support struts.

"That means you are about to be a very busy man, my friend. That means you'll have to dive tonight. Dead right."

"Yeah." Jonas crossed his arms over his barrel chest and leaned against the wall of the cabin; the cool steel of the wall felt good on his bare upper arm. In the television screen he could make out the reflection of his face as he studied the weather map with Bebe. Almost subconsciously he raised his eyebrows in surprise as he notice his own thinning hair and tired eyes. His skin was tanned golden brown, but not nearly as dark as February's. His clean-shaven face was ruddy from years at sea, and its features were roughly chiseled and lined as though carved by some sculptor whose intent was to accentuate the years of experience.

Jonas was not a handsome man, just plain with rough edges. But he had the kind of temperament that drew people to him, a peacefulness in his soul. There was something more to Jonas than just a skilled diver. He had been born in the small Atlantic seaside community of Mystic, Connecticut, where he had always been drawn to the water. Growing up, he frequented the historic seaport and aquarium and learned of the town's whaling history. He had honed his mechanical and welding skills working with fishermen and their boats and soon became an expert diver as well. After college he followed work around the world before landing this prized job on the *Atlantic Stroom* out of Cape Town, South Africa.

"Well, you have fourteen hours by my estimate, maybe a little more."

"Right, then, I'm off. Let me know if things change. I'll be on the lower deck getting ready. I'll try to dive within the hour."

"Very good, Jonas. As always, I'll have you on the screen. Be sure to wave."

"Yeah, see you later."

"Dead right."

Jonas climbed down the myriad of ladders and walked through a series of corridors in order to get to the lower deck of the *Atlantic Stroom*. Finally he undogged a hatch and ducked his head into a spacious workroom that rattled and hummed with activity.

In the center of the room was the black hole—the vertical shaft that provided access to the subsurface structure of the drill platform. Formed by a steel pipe six meters in diameter, it was called a moon pool, and it allowed the divers to go below to perform standard maintenance on the platform's massive pontoons and substructure, even during moderately rough weather if necessary to make emergency repairs. In the older days of open decks, the reflection of the moon could be seen by looking down into the diving well from the ship's mast. But on the *Atlantic Stroom* the well opened up into one of the enclosed and artificially lit lower decks, and because it extended ten meters down to sea level and then another eight meters down into the ocean, the water was typically black. The drill platform provided a cover, casting a shadow and hiding the normal green phosphorous glow of the ocean, hence it was known as the black hole.

"Storm coming in," Jonas said to Willy Drusbury, the *Atlantic Stroom*'s diving captain, at his post in the black hole room. "How far along are you before I can dive?"

"Ah Jonas, Piet and I are ready for ya." Willy Drusbury raised his eyebrows, tipped his head forward slightly, and gave his thinning blond hair a good scratch as if such motion would jog loose any forgotten ideas. His head bobbed in confirmation and looked up at Jonas. Drusbury was originally from Liverpool. His face seemed to hold an expression of constant puzzlement, yet he was a very precise, cautious, and thorough dive master.

Piet Van Rooyen, a short, compact man with black scrambled hair and a ruddy complexion, appeared to have many of the eleven national ethnic groups of South Africa flowing through his veins. Van Rooyen said, "It's a big 'un coming in from below the Cape. I'm ready with the Mutt."

Piet and Willy made a good topside team for Jonas. Piet controlled the remotely operated underwater vehicle, or ROV, and Willy kept track of the winches and life support systems. The bright yellow ROV was suspended above the black hole on a cable, awaiting deployment. It was two meters long and tube-shaped, with bug-eyed lenses on each end affixed to an array of cameras. Pivotable propellers in protective sleeves were mounted port and starboard and on the bottom to give the unmanned mini submarine maneuverability. A three-fingered mechanical arm protruded below the camera lens window at the bow. Piet had painted eyes, ears, and a crazy toothed grin on the ROV and had christened it the Mutt.

"Nearly ready, we've got the supports completed and already lowered down in the black hole. We just need to send a welder unit down, and check out a few more things," Willy said. "The welds you gotta make are shown on these plans here." Willy handed Jonas a plasticized twenty-centimeter-square diagram that he could clip to his dive suit. "Yep, that's about it. Review these, then you can suit up in fifteen, and get wet."

Piet gave Jonas a thumbs up for the ROV deployment and use. Van Rooyen would be driving the ROV, with its powerful mechanical arm, high-resolution low-light cameras, and range-finding sonar system, which would assist Jonas in the dive.

Jonas went into the adjoining diver's changing room and sorted though his gear. He considered the skintight, ten-mil foam wet suit his own personal layer of removable whale blubber. The waters of the South Atlantic were cold, a cold urged northward from the oceans of Antarctica by the lazy Benguela Current. The wet suit was black with yellow bands on the arm and fluorescent red triangles on the back and chest. Jonas first tested the connectors and tubes on what he called his umbilical cord, which would send air to his lungs, heated water to his suit, and communications to his ears. The umbilical was paired with a five-millimeter cable that acted as a safety line should Willy have to pull him up. Satisfied that everything was working, he then rechecked the compressor for the air lines.

Willy Drusbury poked his head in the room and, over the general din of the machinery, said, "Ready Jonas, everything's wet."

"Right, thanks." Jonas stripped down to his swim trunks and stepped into the wet suit. Pulling the tough, elastic rubber suit over his legs took several minutes as he squirmed to get the suit up to his waist. Next, he took a deep breath to puff out his chest and flatten his stomach to pull the suit up over his shoulders and—exhaling—to zip it up to his neck over his muscled chest. Then he stretched a rubberized hood over his head to protect him from the cold water—it fit snug around his cheeks and jaw. Jonas attached the air-communication-suit-warmer umbilical to his dive helmet and held it in his hand. The air regulator was integrated into the dive helmet as a multitasking unit. Then he put on the fins and gloves.

Jonas walked like a duck out of water over to the black hole and peered into the darkness below. He glanced at the lines dangling from the overhead winch as they extended into the blackness. "Hit the lights, will ya, Willy." A string of white, waterproof spots suddenly glowed down the entire inner length of the black hole. The water changed from black and foreboding to green and mysterious. Jonas saw the silvery glint of a small fish several meters down, but other than that the sea as seen from the lower parts of the *Atlantic Stroom* was clear and quiet. Outside, though, the four-meter swell continued to wash around the semi.

Jonas climbed down the side ladder, sat down on the edge of the black hole's launching deck, and dangled his feet over the cold water. He strapped on his dive helmet unit, with the requisite breathing hoses, rechecked his umbilical cable connections, and tested the miniature microphone in the mask. He took several deep sucks of the metallic-tasting air as it hissed into his face mask. Counting aloud to five forward and backward Jonas looked up at Willy, who gave him another thumbs up.

Piet Van Rooyen also waved an okay and Jonas slipped over the side in a sudden upwelling of bubbles and cold water. He could feel the warm water begin to move between the rubber suit and his skin as it flowed down the umbilicus—this would keep him warm for hours. The noise of the machinery vanished into quiet thunks in the water, and soon all Jonas could hear was the distant thumping of low-frequency vibrations from the semi. He relaxed to the regular sound of his breathing. The water always calmed him.

The wet suit that had been so tight and unnatural out of the water now seemed to move with him and keep him warm. The weights on his belt gave him neutral buoyancy, and Jonas swam with practiced ease over to a lead cable that extended through the black hole. He clipped himself onto it with a carabiner. This would guide him to the working area where Willy had lowered the welding gear. Jonas pulled himself down along the cable, trailing his umbilicus.

Slowly the pressure built around Jonas, and he equalized it within his ears and continued his slow progress downward. Soon he was at the lower edge of the pipe, eight meters below sea level, and as he kicked out into the open ocean he could feel the one-knot current grab at him and try to carry him northward.

The semi's starboard pontoon loomed up in front of him like a huge, rusty submarine. The additional bracing had already been lowered into position from the main deck, and the welding torch was dangling free on the end of the cable.

"See me, Piet?"

"Gotcha," replied Piet Van Rooyen, as he deftly turned the tethered ROV toward Jonas. Piet would keep the Mutt near Jonas like it was a loyal pet dog. The wide-angle, low-light video camera on the Mutt gave Piet a full view of the operations, and he could help Jonas inspect work in progress. The video image was also sent up to one of the screens in the weather station where Bebe February worked. Bebe would keep an eye on things as an added backup. The twin bright lights glared at the diver, and Piet steadied the Mutt into place, delicately balancing it in the current. He tested the single mechanical arm, and the three metallic fingers clinched and opened like an alien fist.

The small propellers of the Mutt whirred, and Jonas could hear the high-pitched hum of the electric motors. Like a tethered dog, the machine was always around, always willing to help out on these jobs, and—through Piet—something tangible he could talk to while solving problems underwater. Now the lights from the Mutt illuminated the repair area, and Jonas set to work. "Piet, could you drive the Mutt over here and steady the brace while I fire up the torch?"

"Will do." Piet directed the Mutt's arm as he checked the sonar range finder on the distance and then grasped the metal support beam with a gentle but firm grip. "Got it." In the television screen Piet noticed Jonas glance up at the Mutt to visually confirm what he had heard in his earphone. Piet nodded in silent approval from his topside console—when in the drink, one always confirmed things for oneself; it was how you stayed alive. Jonas was as good as they came. The screen flared slightly as Jonas lit the underwater welding torch.

Jonas moved slowly into position alongside the massive pontoon as the torch sparked with a muffled, aqueous crackle. Although the metal looked fine to the human eye, earlier ultrasound testing by the Mutt indicated metal fatigue along one of the main support welds. Jonas lowered the welder's tinted shield on his diver's helmet. His task was simply to reinforce the weld with several strips of steel before anything failed. This would take a few hours, and these hours passed slowly. Jonas concentrated on the task at hand, carefully packing in the weld so that the join would be uniform and strong.

About halfway through the job he took an underwater break to stretch his arms. "Taking a short one, Piet."

"Okay," came the tinny reply in Jonas's earphone. "You were at it for quite a while, how do you feel?"

"Fine. You know it's nicer down here than topside!" Jonas swam slowly along the eighty-meter-long pontoon with his umbilical cable trailing behind. There were two such pontoons on the *Atlantic Stroom*—starboard and port. Each pontoon had three support legs that kept the drilling platform above water. The pontoons were neutrally buoyed so they would sit twenty meters below the ocean's surface. This was below the wave base, except for the most massive of waves, and that kept the platform relatively motion free. As Jonas swam along his mind wandered in the murky water. It was nighttime topside and very dark below. His hand lamp, strapped to his wrist, tracked along the pontoon only as a point of reference. Jonas had a second lamp on his helmet. Now and then a small silvery fish would flash in the artificial light and be gone. The light also reflected and illuminated the small phytoplankton that welled up in the cold water. This gave the murkiness a dusty quality.

Having swam half the length of the pontoon, Jonas turned around and started back to his workstation. The steady pumping of his legs and the rhythmic breathing were his mantra. Even as the one-knot current pushed against him, Jonas sensed the subtle changes of pressure in the water caused by other animals. The mammals of the sea, the big fish, and the behemoths. He looked around half expecting to see the dolphin that had been watching him earlier, but it was nowhere to be found. Yet he could sense a presence in the water. It was undefinable, yet real, as if hearing a noise in the woods or feeling the whoosh of air overhead as a bird passes close. Soon though he was back at his workstation and once again welding the joins.

The glare and spark of his welding torch gave a false, nervous light to the dark world below the *Atlantic Stroom*. The flurry of bubbles around him popped and crackled as they cavitated and rose to the surface like wobbling silvery jellyfish. The glare of the Mutt's lamp illuminated the scene with strange, flat lighting and washed out the scene to a dark gray-green spectrum. Jonas's face mask gave him a tunnel view of the aqueous world, with visibility only possible by artificial light. The heavily tinted visor over his face mask while welding, in combination with the muffled noises from his work, fairly well isolated him from his immediate surroundings. He vaguely sensed the shadow that passed in front of the Mutt's lights.

"Jonas, you okay?" came Piet's voice through the earphone.

"I'm fine, what's up?" replied Jonas, as he looked up from his work. The sea was dark through the tinted visor, so he turned down the welding torch, which continued to bubble nervously, and then lifted the visor. Everything seemed all right as he scanned his surroundings.

"Some fish just swam in front of the Mutt, I was wondering if you saw it."

"No. Had my visor down." Jonas continued to look around. "Big or small?"

"Medium, maybe big," said Piet. "On the video it was just one of those nondescript gray streaks, could have been anything from a tuna to a whale. Well, not as big as a whale, according to the Mutt's sonar, but not too small." On the Mutt's sonar Piet could see the fast-moving fish as it swam around the work area. "I'm looking at the sonar, Jonas, and it's kinda big. It's moving away now." The pontoon showed up on the sonar screen as a massive line of white dots on the green screen, while Jonas was trackable as a small composite of dots.

"Well, keep me informed," replied Jonas, as he turned back to his work. He faced the rusty gray-brown pontoon wall, which rose many meters above him—a steel barrier in the black ocean. He looked up the wall and watched the air bubbles from the expiration valve on his headgear disappear into the darkness like fleeting thoughts. Suddenly within the limits of the lights he saw a gray form streak past the pontoon. "Just saw it, Piet."

"And?"

"Don't know, not too big though. There it is again, hey, it's a dolphin!" Jonas smiled into his face mask as he felt the adrenaline subside, having determined what the gray streak really was. "He's swimming circles around the Mutt."

Once in a while Piet could see the gray form streak in front of the Mutt's camera, but the animal was fast, and he couldn't tell it was a dolphin. He tried to follow it by spinning the Mutt around, but the dolphin was just too fast. "Seems to be camera shy, Jonas."

"Yeah, well, he may just be playing with the Mutt. It is pretty lonely down here." Jonas watched the dolphin pass in and out of the light, streaking off into the murky water only to reappear moments later from another angle. It was a good-sized one, with it's distinctive jutting lower jaw, beautifully curved dorsal fin, and horizontal flukes. In a flash the right side of the dolphin came into Jonas's view, and he could clearly see the distinctive markings he'd seen before. "Hey, Piet, this is the dancer, the one that sometimes leaps around the platform."

"What's he doing here all alone at night?"

"No idea, Piet. Hey!" Jonas yelled into his microphone as the dolphin seemed to charge forward directly at him. Jonas could see it's grinning face appearing suddenly, only veering away at the last moment. He could feel the push of water from the dolphin passing so close. "This one just charged me!"

"Playing?"

"Maybe, can't see him now, but it didn't seem like he was playing. I've met up with dolphins before, and they usually just ignore divers." Suddenly the dolphin rushed by Jonas a second time, but even closer. He could just feel one of its flippers graze his arm as he brought it up to fend off the crazy beast. Jonas's mind seemed to spark with the dolphin's touch, as sudden and fleeting images of the ocean flashed through his consciousness. He shook his head to clear it. "That was close, I don't know what's up with this one, but it's definitely in harassment mode." He shook his head again, refusing to believe the hallucinations he had just briefly experienced.

Piet steered the Mutt closer to Jonas and spoke into his microphone. "Maybe I can place the Mutt between you and your friend."

"Yeah, that might work."

"Or do you want to come up for a spell and let this fish go on about its way? Willy can pull you up pretty fast on your line."

"No, Bebe said the storm will be here tomorrow, so I want to get this welded tonight. I want you and the Mutt to have enough time to do some ultrasonics and recheck the welds. No, gotta be done now."

"Okay," Piet said as he watched the gray streak pass the Mutt's camera again. "Your friend is back."

Jonas looked to his right just in time to see the dolphin swim by again. But this time it circled around with a thrust from its flukes and faced Jonas directly. It pumped its tail to keep itself stationary in the lazy current. "So, what do you want my friend?" Jonas whispered to himself.

"Come again?" interrupted Piet. He had trained the Mutt's camera on Jonas and was watching the dolphin watch the diver. "What's going on down there, Jonas?"

"I don't know, Piet, this fella is just watching me." The front view of a dolphin is a curious one, and Jonas almost chuckled aloud at the scene. The apparent smile and the small, slightly forward-looking eyes set back on the sides of the bulbous head offer a peculiar view. The dolphin's eyes worked independently of each other as it studied him. He watched the animal with rapt curiosity. The dolphin nodded and then shook his head and suddenly darted upward along Jonas's umbilical cable. All the years Jonas had been at sea and on all the thousands of dives he'd taken, he'd never experienced a dolphin interacting with a diver this way. He wondered if it was a tame dolphin that had escaped captivity. He wondered if he was just reading too much into the behavior— what did they call it, anthropomorphizing?

The dolphin swam back down the cable and abruptly turned around and repeated its ascent. It did it two more times as Jonas watched in continued amazement. "Hey, Piet, we've got a real star here, a real performer!"

"What's it doing? All I can see in the monitor is the occasional gray streak except when you two were having the old face to face."

Jonas explained what the dolphin was doing. Again it returned to face him and repeated the nod and wag of its head. Puzzled, Jonas reached out toward the dolphin. This caused a commotion, and the dolphin swam in a rapid vertical circle and then suddenly lunged forward, its beak just touching Jonas's outstretched hand.

The delicate contact sent sparks of emotions through Jonas. He flailed back in the water and withdrew his hand. His entire being was suddenly overcome with intense fear. *What's this all about*, he wondered to himself. He could feel uncontrollable panic starting to build in his system. He fought to keep it down, but even so his breathing increased, and he looked around wildly. His arms and legs flailed again with indecision as to which direction to swim. These sudden and erratic motions were not lost on Piet, who continued to monitor the scene.

"Hey, buddy, what's up?" Piet asked in a clear, level tone. He recognized panic when he saw it but could see no reason for the actions. The dolphin was gone, and Jonas seemed to be floundering.

Willy looked over Piet's shoulder and watched the video monitor. "You okay, Jonas?"

Jonas responded in rushed, breathy words, "I don't know, I don't know, that—a, dolphin, I don't know, there is something, ah, gotta get up fast, there is something!"

"What? What? Jonas, speak to me, what's there, are you hurt?"

"I'm bringing him up," Willy shouted.

"No. Not hurt. Don't know the words for it, I just . . ."

"You okay, buddy?" Piet asked again in a very even tone.

"Yeah, yeah, I just . . . yeah I'm all right." Jonas's breathing had slowed somewhat, but there was still a panicky edge to his voice. "See anything with the Mutt or sonar?"

"Bring him up, let's bring him up," Willy said again.

Piet studied the sonar screen on his console. The radially sweeping line mapped out the pontoon and Jonas's location. Nothing else was visible. "No, Jonas, I don't see anything else, just you and the semi. Your friend is also gone. There's nothing there, Jonas."

"Yes, there is. I can *feel* it."

"You gotta come up man, I agree with Willy; we're pulling you up."

"Wait, Piet, I have to figure this one out." Jonas paused as he searched for the right words. He didn't want to sound crazy, and now that the panicky feeling had subsided he chose his words with reasoned care. "That dolphin touched my hand, and I, it was like, I could feel it. I *can* feel it . . ."

"Well, if it touched you, of course you could feel it," Piet said, puzzled by Jonas's words. He looked over at Willy with raised eyebrows and motioned to the winch console. "Look, I'm gonna have Willy pull you up, you don't have to swim or nothing. Your cable is plenty strong, you just enjoy the ride. Okay?"

Before Jonas could answer a shape loomed up in front of him, and his sudden intake of breath was sharp and raspy in Piet's headphones topside. At the same instant the huge form passed between Jonas and the Mutt's camera. All Piet and Willy could see on the video monitor was a huge gray form with a dorsal fin. All Jonas could see was a mouth full of ragged teeth.

It was a great white shark.

"Willy, pull him up!"

"NO!" yelled Jonas. "Great white!" If they pulled him up now, the move would land him right into the jaws of the shark. He kicked hard and fast backward and slammed into the massive wall of the pontoon. It was just enough motion to avoid the jaws of the shark. Jonas was breathing heavily and frantically looking around, for the shark had vanished in the dark murk of the ocean. "Sonar! Piet, where is it?"

"I'm not sure, it could be along the pontoon, or above you." Piet was sweating, and Willy had his hand on the cable controls. "Let Willy pull you up!"

"No, not until I know where it is. Christ, it's a big one!" Jonas's senses tingled from fear laced with adrenaline. He could see Piet moving the ROV around trying to visually scan the area.

It was back. The huge scarred form of the great white shark swam out of the darkness directly toward Jonas. The rhythmic back-and-forth wagging of the shark's body was almost hypnotic, but Jonas now saw only death in the primitive motion. The oncoming shark looked like a wall of teeth as wide as a car. As the motions quickened, time seemed to slow. Jonas pumped his legs, they felt like lead moving through a molasses ocean compared to the effortless advance of the shark. Jonas gulped air as his muscles strained against the ocean current. In a microsecond he saw the protective white cover close over the shark's nearest eye—it was the behemoth's war cry. He watched in weird slow-motion horror as the jaws parted and gapped, the teeth seemed to jut outward toward his legs. He pumped hard. Jonas watched in fascinated abhorrence—as if he was an observer, not a participant in the unraveling events—as the rows of teeth began to close on his right leg.

In an eruption of bubbles and turmoil Jonas was slammed against the metallic wall of the pontoon, but it wasn't from the shark's attack. He felt the rigid, angled frame of the ROV—his undersea companion, the Mutt—pinning him against the pontoon's wall. The outstretched mechanical arm was between Jonas and the shark, and he watched as the white razors clamped down on the metal.

In frustrated surprise and fury the shark tore and snapped at the mechanical arm, shaking it twice before releasing it. The shark turned abruptly away and circled off into the darkness.

"Jonas!" yelled Piet into the diver's earphone, "hang onto the Mutt, we're pulling you up right now and fast!" Piet yelled over to Willy to make sure the decompression chamber was ready to receive Jonas.

Jonas didn't argue, he just clung to the yellow metal frame of the Mutt. He could feel several tentative tugs as the excess slack in the cables was taken up and the winches took hold. He was yanked away from the imposing wall of the pontoon and into the dark water. He could feel the pull of the ocean around him as the winches accelerated. Jonas's head jerked from right to left in search of the shark, for his senses told him it was close and would not give up easily—evolution wouldn't allow it. He did not have long to wait for its return.

The hulking form of the shark seemed to glow an iridescent gray in the wake of the ROV to which Jonas clung. The speed of the winches caused bubbles to form around the steel frame and these enveloped Jonas, reflecting back like mercury tears in the high-intensity lights of the Mutt.

"Willy, step on it!"

Willy leaned into the cable lift controls.

Piet turned the camera aft and saw what Jonas was watching. He called to Willy, who yelled back that the motors were at full. The shark seemed to gnash its teeth as if anticipating imminent contact—it *needed* to catch its prey, Jonas could sense this. The shark matched the speed of the ROV—and Jonas—then began closing the distance. Jonas could sense the enveloping walls of the vertical well—the black hole. He had a fleeting memory of an astronomer saying nothing ever gets out of a black hole once it has gone in. Jonas had entered the black hole. He would find out soon an astronomer's prophecy.

The lights topside illuminated the surrounding water to an emerald green color. Jonas looked up and could see his air bubbles breaking the surface, he looked down at the gaping jaws of the shark. He couldn't believe the thing had followed him up the well.

The Mutt and Jonas broke the surface of the water with an eruption of foam and spray that echoed hollowly in the chamber. The cables yanked him two meters clear of the water as Willy rammed on the brakes to stop Jonas from smashing into the pulleys.

The shark rocketed out of the water, straight up at Jonas, its ugly maw clamping shut on the diving fin strapped to his right foot. Jonas felt the elastic stretch and then something gave, and the behemoth fell back into the well. It turned and dove back into the black hole from whence it came.

CHAPTER

3

You cannot turn the wind, so turn your sail.
Namibian proverb

Bebe February rubbed his chin and looked at his old friend. For him it had been a long, long day, and one which had almost seen the end of Jonas. Bebe liked the man. Jonas had always treated him as a brother; they had stood together when others would have turned away or pointed a finger. Bebe smiled inwardly and said in a low, scolding voice, "Do not try to fight a lion if you are not one yourself."

"Hey, Bebe, I wasn't trying to fight anything down there, it was trying to eat me!" Jonas held out his diving flipper as further proof—proof that Bebe February didn't really need. The end of the flipper was ragged, ripped by the shark's teeth. For Jonas the day had passed quickly, because the adrenaline subsided only very slowly. Others on the *Atlantic Stroom* came around to get a firsthand description of what happened. Jonas showed them the ragged shark-torn flipper and the huge shark's tooth that had been wedged in the cardan joint of the Mutt's mechanical arm. The tooth looked like that of an ancient megalodon shark it was so big. Finally, though, he retreated to the weather room to chat with Bebe and find out the status of the approaching storm.

"Yes, that's its nature. But it must have thought you were a challenge, for what one shark does, all sharks do," said Bebe February, seriously, as he fingered the shark's tooth. It was very large and jagged and easily filled the palm of his big hand.

"What does that mean? I think it just saw an easy catch, and thanks to Piet and Willy's fast responses, all it got was a broken tooth."

"So, tell me of this dolphin."

"The one that charged me?"

"The same. I talked to Piet, and he says it was swimming all around you like it was crazy. So, tell me of this dolphin," Bebe said again.

Jonas ran a hand over his head to smooth his hair as he thought of what to say. He didn't know anything. "It must have been freaked out by that shark and then just confused by the lights around the Mutt."

"But it came *at* you. And it did so again and again," Bebe said. "It knew it could warn you and was obviously troubled by your situation. Now Jonas, you can't teach the dolphin how to swim."

Jonas smiled at another of his friend's sayings, and said, "What's that supposed to mean, Bebe. You and all these Namib riddles." Jonas knocked him in the shoulder playfully with a soft fist. "I don't know, maybe the dolphin really was trying to warn me. After all, they are known to help people from time to time."

"True enough. So it was helping you—I believe it. So should you." Bebe smiled broadly and nodded slowly, mimicking the attitude of the wise elders of his village. It was a practiced and conscious gesture.

Jonas had to finish the task abandoned when the shark attacked him. So he and another diver spent two more hours welding on the pontoon. Jonas kept a vigilant eye on the murky waters should the shark return. The storm's estimated time of arrival had been pushed back a couple hours. His nerves had been rattled by the shark, but when he actually got back in the water he felt comforted, and now and then he caught a glimpse of his dolphin friend. Piet Van Rooyen also kept a close watch on them with the Mutt and came to recognize the distinctive motions and shape of the dolphin on his sonar scope. He'd say, "It's just your friend again, nothing to worry about."

Willy considered the recent events with a sober nod. He furrowed his brow and decided to touch base with the weather room. He called Bebe over the intercom and said, "Keep keeping your eyes on our man." Bebe assured Willy he could think of nothing else.

Jonas was exhausted by the time he broke the water's surface in the moon pool. As he sat with the other diver on the metal stoop rimming the pool, he could feel the sea's rolling waves sending shudders through the *Atlantic Stroom*. They glanced at each other as they removed the heavy gear, knowing that their repairs would be tested soon enough.

The captain ordered the semi ballasted for storm survival. This meant that the pontoons would be allowed to rise slightly from their twenty-one-meter draft up to a sixteen-meter draft. This would continue to give the floating drill platform stability in the water, but at the same time maintain a greater air gap of fifteen meters between the main deck and the sea surface. In this way the building waves would not wash over the deck. It was a compromise between the operating draft and transit draft to assure the safety of the semi. It worked as long as waves greater than fifteen meters did not pound the platform. As a safety precaution valves were closed and circuits switched off for some of the in-pontoon functions.

The Force 9 storm enveloped the *Atlantic Stroom* and the western coast of Namibia for three solid days. It soaked the desert in the days that followed. The normally sere landscape exploded in wildflower blossoms in response to the rare and welcome income of landfall precipitation.

Meanwhile, on the *Atlantic Stroom*, Jonas's welding held firm. He received many congratulatory claps on the back for his work, often accompanied by a shark joke.

In the wake of the storm Jonas received a note from the company's general manager in Cape Town, Johan Van Stuer. The note congratulated him on the fine repairs and a job well done so that the *Atlantic Stroom* would weather yet another storm. Van Stuer also remarked on the shark adventure, as he called it, and urged Jonas to take care, since a diver and employee of Jonas's caliber was a valued member of the company's family.

Jonas showed Bebe the note, and Bebe had commented that praise from above was usually a good thing. Nevertheless, it was a nice accolade.

When the storm finally subsided, the veteran drilling team fell right back into the routine of drilling for oil. The sea became unseasonably calm and for a solid day was mirror-like.

Jonas climbed down the access ladder on the aft starboard support leg. It was a massive cylinder of steel, one of six, which supported the 2,590-square-meter deck on the two eighty-meter-long pontoons. There was a walkaround mooring deck welded one meter above operational ballast height. Jonas sat there now, bare feet dangling above the water as he gazed out over the mirror sea in the late afternoon. He was off for a day, and his only goal was to sit there and watch the sunset—it would be a three-hour wait, one he relished.

Suddenly Jonas's daydreaming was broken by a swash of water near his feet. He instantly recognize the distinctive rosebush thorn shape of a dolphin's dorsal fin cutting through the water by the mooring deck.

"Ha!" Jonas yelled, "You've come back, my friend, to scare the sharks away!"

The dolphin dove beneath the surface and then rocketed upward in a spectacular leap—five meters into the air, spinning twice and then slapping the water and soaking Jonas.

"You rascal! I needed a bath anyway," Jonas roared again, laughing long and hard. It was a release to see this dolphin. He couldn't explain it, but his cares slipped away, and he felt an elation he'd never experienced before.

The dolphin swam to the surface again and let out a noisy series of chatterings and went racing around the aft starboard support leg. It then slowed and nodded its head and beak below Jonas's feet. Jonas clamored around and lay on his stomach, reaching a hand down to touch the dolphin.

The dolphin moved closer and nuzzled Jonas's hand. As Jonas touched the dolphin's beak he was suddenly overcome with emotion. He jerked his hand back as if he'd received a shock. Eyes wide with surprise, he tentatively reached down again for the waiting dolphin. Again his senses were flooded with emotion and realization.

"How can this be?" Jonas asked, although he had not spoken. Somehow his thoughts were communicated directly to the dolphin, as were the dolphin's to him.

"It is, that is all," Peek said.

"But I can understand you! You saved me from that shark, why?"

"That shark, that is Old Death and known by no other name. He has been here longer than any dolphin can remember, and he hates humans. He hates dolphins. He hates seals. Old Death even attacks whales sometimes. I could not let you succumb to Old

Death. You must remember how he moved and be more ready next time," Peek said.

"But how did you know the shark was after me?"

"We sounded your fear."

"What? But I saw you before the shark arrived."

"Did you? Did you suspect something in the dark water. Did you not pause and consider subtle vibrations that did not seem familiar . . . friendly?" Peek asked.

"Hmm, now that you mention it, I do recall wondering if something was out there. But you came so fast."

"Yes. Because I knew Old Death was about, and I knew you had detected him—even if it was subconsciously. When in the ocean always trust your instincts."

"I am still puzzled by this, our minds seem to understand each other. You seem to be smart."

"What did you expect? Of course, I'm smart. One's got to be smart to live a long life in these waters. You should know that, you're smart," Peek said. "Besides, did you think man was the only intelligent animal in the oceans?"

"Well, we seem to be it on the land," Jonas said. His hand was still outstretched and rested on Peek's beak.

"Are you sure? Before this instant you thought man was the smartest everywhere."

"That's true, but I mean, mankind builds things and has relationships and travels and keeps track of time and all that stuff."

"And you think that I, as what you call a dolphin, don't travel and have relationships? Of course, we don't build things like you, but we also don't pollute the oceans like you do. Which is better? Which is smarter?"

"I, uh, I don't know. I mean that's what man does. We build things."

"Does building things mean you're smarter? The coral builds things—you call them reefs. The seabirds build things—you call them nests. I don't need to build things to do what I do. I like to explore the oceans. I fancy myself as a full-time explorer. I have seen many things. I can find food anywhere and don't need one of those loud things you float in to travel on the water."

"Oh, yeah, boats."

"Those boats, as you call them, bite at us if we get too near. It's fun to ride the wave in front, but we have to keep the young from swimming underneath. The boats bite us," Peek said.

"Those are the propellers. They push the boat forward like you swim with your flukes. They aren't alive, they're just part of one of our machines we call motors. You've heard them, I know, because I can hear them when I'm underwater. It's that growling sound or a deep, repetitive *shush shush shush.*"

"That last sound, that's from the really big boats."

"Those are the oil tankers and cargo container boats."

"Sometimes they excrete that foul-tasting black poison that kills the fish and sticks to the seabirds."

"That's the oil, which feeds the machines you hear. That is why I am here on this drilling rig, to fix things so others can drill for oil to run our machines."

"Some also shed tough clear skin. We get tangled in it some-times. It can be deadly, but we are learning about it."

"Plastic. Yes, it's everywhere now. Not only in the oceans, but mankind seems to have dropped it everywhere on land and sea," Jonas said. He felt embarrassed, even a bit ashamed of his species behavior.

"Do you need these machines? Do you need this plastic? Do you need this oil?"

"Yes," Jonas said. "These things drive our civilization. I guess that doesn't make much sense to you."

"I understand the thought. My civilization is mobile. We swim in home families."

"Shoals and pods. Man has named a group of dolphins a shoal of dolphins, at least down here in South Africa and Namibia, and a group of whales is a pod of whales."

"Okay. But we call them home families. I don't care what you call us because I know what we are. And our civilization doesn't need machines. We are the explorers of the oceans, like the whales."

"That's amazing. I've never thought of it that way," Jonas said. He suddenly realized he was getting used to this way of conversing. But he found it difficult to continue to focus his thoughts—they wanted to wander, there was so much to ask. Part of him thought he was still just daydreaming, another part accepted it and felt comfort and companionship in it—the emotions were so natural, yet so new. "But why can I talk to you? Am I suppose to do something?"

"Yes. I think so. This is almost as much a surprise to me as to you. I felt driven to seek you out and talk to you."

"Why? Why do you have to talk to me?"

"I don't know."

"But I wasn't looking for you," Jonas said.

"I know that," said the dolphin. "You were not looking, and that is why I found you. But I must go now."

"Your name, what do your friends call you?" Jonas asked.

"I am called Peek because that is what I have always been called. And you are my friend, I can tell, so you can call me Peek."

"I am Jonas. Jonas Jeremy James is what I've always been called." Jonas still rested his hand on the Peek's beak, and indeed it would have looked an odd sight if someone on the main deck had peered over and seen them.

"But I must go now," Peek said again.

"Why?"

"Because of the sunset, of course."

Jonas puzzled over that for a moment and asked, "Do you go somewhere after sunset?"

"Oh, no, not that at all. We love to watch the sunset, so me and my friends have a game—we all try to leap into the dry blue just as the sun touches the ocean. Sometimes we seem to do this just as a green flash occurs when the sun dips low. It's a game from childhood, and we invented it because we noticed the sun always changes color and the air grows cooler as it goes down. So the game is to jump out of the water to catch the last warmth before the ocean puts out the light."

"Wow," Jonas said slowly. It had never occurred to him that a dolphin would play games with the sun. And the fact that the dolphins watch the sunset and had seen the uncommon optical phenomenon called the green ray or green flash was remarkable.

"So I must be wet and fast to meet them. You can watch us, just look toward the sun and wait until it touches the sea."

With that, Peek slipped beneath the mirror ocean with barely a ripple. The conversation was cut off like someone slamming a door. Jonas sat up on the walkaround deck. He felt as if he'd been slapped in the face when the contact was broken. *Unbelievable!* He thought to himself. Jonas saw the distinctive dorsal fin surface moments later in west—toward the sun.

The sun dipped low, and Jonas didn't take his eyes off the horizon for fear of missing the dolphins. The blue water darkened and the horizon reddened and the sun seemed to swell grander in it's daily valediction. Suddenly, about a kilometer distant, just as the sun seemed to melt into the water as a shimmering disc, Jonas saw no less than twenty dolphins launch themselves from the ocean and flip over in unison. All were silhouetted by the red sunset in a spectacular aerial show that lasted only seconds. Just then he saw the fabled green flash, occurring as a green spot at the top of the molten, orange-red sun. The dolphins fell back to the sea in a riot of splashes and scattered like raindrops on a ship's deck.

Jonas sat there alone well into the night. It was with great reluctance that he left the ocean side and climbed the metal ladder up to the main deck and civilization. *Human civilization,* he corrected himself.

From the main deck Bebe February had watched the curious, apparently silent communication between Jonas and the dolphin. After a time he left Jonas to himself and went off to ponder what he had seen.

CHAPTER

4

The tortoise is the wisest;
he carries his own home.
Namibian proverb

Madeleine James sat in her four-room apartment in Mystic, Connecticut, and read the letter she had just received from her brother. Her long, straight, black hair fell around her slender face as she rested her chin on her hand. It was a contemplative pose, and her face held a curious and disbelieving expression. It was the fourth time she'd read the letter, and each time it had moved her more and worried her more. The schoolteacher in her was looking for hidden meanings in the descriptive phases Jonas had sent her.

She paused and looked out the window. She resided in the small village in a studio apartment above the shops on West Main Street, less than a block from the historic drawbridge. The town was somewhat magical—well, she chuckled to herself, somewhat mystical—because of its links to the sea, its tall ships and historic seaport and research aquarium. All of it along the Mystic River, and all of it keeping the ocean always in her mind. She and her brother had grown up here.

Was Jonas going crazy after all these years working far and wide on various desolate drill platforms? Had two decades at sea finally gotten to him? Was he hallucinating, talking to fish? Was he telling the truth? The letter seemed rational, but Jonas had clearly been very excited about what had happened and had written her the same evening. She reread the last paragraph:

Finally, you must not think I've lost it, sis. I am writing to you because I have to tell someone. But no one on board the Atlantic Stroom, *except maybe Bebe—you remember him, I've written you about Bebe from Namibia—would even let me get a sentence out before laughing. But I tell you this: I am sane, and I did talk to a dolphin. It's magic, Maddy, it's absolute magic.*

The next day Madeleine was distracted. She taught fifth grade at one of the public schools and found she could not concentrate on the lessons. The kids laughed at her apparent absentminded-ness, and one girl even yelled out: "Miss James is in *love . . .*"

That evening Madeleine decided to drive to the beach, to flee the lights of the city—not an easy task on the Eastern Seaboard. But the night was clear, and she had to see the stars. As she made her way along the curves of the road and past the vintage homes from the 1800s, the quaint markets, and small patches of forest and wetlands, she thought of her life here in this one place. She thought of how Jonas had seen the world, while she had seen to the education of hundreds of young children over the decades he'd been at sea. She heard the mournful horn of the Amtrak train as it crossed the bridge at Beebe Cove. Odd that the name of the cove was so similar to her brother's overseas friend. Nothing happens by accident, she thought.

She turned southeast to cross the tracks into the small lobster and fishing town of Noank, just a few miles southwest of Mystic. The small-town lights glowed, and the seaside homes were warmly lit. Driving her car on the all but empty roads, she finally pulled up to the small public dock on the beach at the end of Main Street and shut off the engine. Madeleine peered out through the windshield and then hurriedly opened the car door and got out. She looked up at the dome of stars above her as they spread out over the North Atlantic: countless beacons smeared across a black palette. She recalled an old phrase from a book she had once read: *the candles that guide the ships.*

"My God, it is beautiful," Madeleine whispered to herself. The hours slipped by as she watched the stars and considered her life and her brother. She felt an odd connection with Jonas when she came to this spot—for she knew it was already the beginnings of a new day for him on the other side of the same ocean and on the other side of the equator.

Madeleine felt she needed to connect with Jonas. They were very close, and his choice to go to sea long ago had not diminished their closeness. But now something new was happening to him, and she had to reach out to him somehow. Madeleine had brought a star chart home from her classroom and studied it. Now she looked up to search for the constellations she had come to the seashore to find. Something was drawing her to try to understand everything about what Jonas was experiencing. There, near the Swan and the Eagle and the Great Bear, were the ten stars that made up Delphinus.

"Delphinus," Madeleine said aloud. The Greeks believed Delphi to be the center of the world. Apollo, the god of light and a patron of Delphi, mimicked the form of a dolphin to appear before mankind. Madeleine hugged herself against the chill of the night, yet she felt warm inside.

"*Delphys,*" Madeleine said in a whisper. It made sense that the ancients had equated the center of the world with the womb: *delphys.* They believed that the dolphin had embodied life and light.

Madeleine had never seen a dolphin, not even at an aquarium. They had beluga whales at the Mystic Aquarium, but no dolphins, at least not the last time she'd been there. The aquarium rescued many sea mammals, and perhaps some had been dolphins. But there were none there now, and she was glad about that. So the dolphins seemed unreal to her, like so much of the world—for she had traveled so very little and had never ventured onto the sea. She thought it was odd that Jonas had discovered a life at sea, while she had only ever been on the boats that motor out from the Old Mystic Seaport—the sunset cruises. Those were the only times she'd been on salt water. She loved the sea, the proximity of it, but from the shore. Yet Jonas had learned how to be at home on the water and especially in the water, no matter where he worked. He had once joked to her that he simply carried his home around with him in his head. Madeleine was sure she could never live the way Jonas did. Shaking her head slightly, she found herself surprised at this realization.

Her thoughts drifted again to her brief research that afternoon about dolphins and their lore, and—as the mind often does—she merged realizations and legends and myths together to form a thought: maybe Jonas was talking so much of dolphins because he was a traveler. A mariner and an explorer—that was Jonas. The early people of the Nabataean civilization in what is now Palestine believed that the dolphin would watch over travelers on land and sea to ensure safe passage. Some even believed they would accompany humans on the grand and final uncharted journey—the one to the great blue yonder.

Madeleine looked up to the stars again and found Delphinus. She spoke aloud, asking the constellation, "Why did you leap to the stars?" To herself she wondered if this had happened, mythically, to escape the thoughtless persecution by mankind? Or was the old Greek storyteller Herodotus right? She recounted the story in her mind.

There was a rich musician and poet in Tarentum named Arion who wished to return to his home of Corinth, from which he'd been away a great long while. To make the voyage he hired a ship, but the crew was evil, for when they learned of Arion's wealth they plotted to take it from him and kill him. Arion discovered the plot and begged the cutthroat crew to allow him to sing and play his lyre one last time.

Well, Arion was famous for his skills, and even the barbaric crew knew it. They wanted to hear the legendary musician play before they killed him, so Arion sang. It was a haunting solemn hymn. He made a heartrending sight for any person of passion as he stood on the deck in his ornately embroidered tunic. The music did not change the heart of the crew, though, and when Arion finished singing they threw him into the waves.

A dolphin, possibly listening to the music as it swam alongside the boat, caught Arion before he could sink beneath the water. Clinging to the back of the dolphin, Arion was transported to shore, from which point he could continue his journey to Corinth. Upon arriving home and being very thankful to the dolphin, Arion wrote a hymn of thanks and praise and love to his rescuer and sang it to the god of the seas, Poseidon. Poseidon, of course, knew of the kindness dolphins show toward all other creatures. To further acknowledge this, and so that all mankind could learn of the true heart of the dolphin, the god of the sea placed its form in the heavens.

Madeleine did not want to leave the shore—it seemed so timeless and exotic in the midnight darkness. She could not shake the feeling that something—for better or worse she could not tell for sure—was happening to her brother. Mythology was all well and good, but reality was unpredictable and held life-changing consequences. She did not know what to do. Madeleine finally gave in to the late hour and returned to her car to drive back to civilization.

CHAPTER

5

There is plenty of water in paradise.
Namibian proverb

Peek was having fun. He loved to chase after the leviathans—the great kings of the sea—the whales. He could hear their cacophony as they rounded up fish. Peek couldn't contain his joy and excitement, and he pumped his flukes to give himself rocket speed. Leaping out of the water a full five meters, Peek spiraled and scanned the horizon in front of him. There, a five-minute swim away, were the humpback whales: circling and circling and circling. The water had become a churning mass of waves and bubbles and anchovies! Peek pumped harder and soon the noise was all around him in the form of huge, dark gray, black and white, slow-motion shapes.

Each whale was distinctive in sight and sound to Peek. He could see the different subtle patterns of white and black on the long pectoral fins and the unique undulations of the waveform tails. All of the humpbacks had tubercles, or knobby areas that were actually hair follicles, on their heads and lower jaws. Some of the males would sing their sonorous melodies for many minutes, and this was a comfort to the pod and friendly sealife. Peek knew many of their names, for these whales migrated far and wide in their lifetimes. The humpbacks were here to feed on their way north to the subtropical breeding grounds off the coast of the continent. They had been summering in the cold krill-laden waters of Antarctica. They made their 20,000-kilometer journey every year, and Peek had seen this pod before.

The humpbacks swam in circles under the huge shoaling school of anchovies and blew bubbles. This made a wall, a bubble net around the fish, which confused them and drove them upward toward the surface. The stupid fish feared the wall of bubbles. Upon reaching the surface, they jumped and leaped as if to leave the ocean altogether—now trapped by air on all sides. The humpbacks tightened their circle and opened their great maws, collecting the small fish in their tight rows of baleen plates. As the whales closed their cavernous mouths, seawater was shushed out between the keratin sheaths of baleen. In this way the humpbacks casually fed on the disoriented and helpless fish. Peek joined in and swam among the humpbacks, helping himself to fish left and right. The humpbacks didn't mind, there were so many, and besides they liked having the dolphins around. Peek could tell because the higher ocean mammals could communicate using not only vocalizations but a crude form of telepathy. This only worked with the most intelligent of mammals. Peek thought briefly that it was odd he could communicate with only one human.

Soon other dolphins swarmed in among the humpbacks to join Peek in the free feast. Thousands of anchovies were gobbled up by hungry dolphins and whales. Dolphins feed by rushing into a school of fish and grabbing and swallowing anything they can reach, so there was a near frenzy of activity. Peek sensed a message from the old female who looked after this pod of whales: *feast and enjoy, my friend, but warn us in the future should you see a whaling boat or the orcas.* Peek and the other dolphins let out a series of whistles and clicks, which thanked the whales and assured them of their constant help and vigilance.

Peek loved to help other animals. It was innate. He understood the reason for this, because of the almost euphoric feeling he experienced when he helped a baby whale to the surface, protected a seal from a shark, or towed a sailor toward the beach. Peek loved moving through the water, loved the feel of it washing over his skin. Coming to the aid of someone in the ocean and propelling them through the water accentuated that feeling. It was an emotional magnification process. All dolphins had this, but some more than others. Peek had plenty and sought out people and other mammals to help should they need it. Certainly some dolphins fought or behaved erratically, for after all, they were just being mammals.

But humans rarely helped dolphins, and this was one reason Peek had sought out Jonas.

Jonas lay on his stomach on the mooring deck again, his hand resting lightly on Peek's beak. "I'm glad you came back, it's been almost a week."

"A week?" Peek asked.

"Yes, a long time. Ah, like the Native American Indians used to say: seven suns."

"I understand the meaning. But who are these other people, these natives?"

"People that originally lived where I come from across the ocean. People that other people tried to chase away."

"Like humans do to whales? Like humans do to dolphins when the fishing boats are around?" Peek asked.

"Yes, something like that." Jonas thought of the whaling heritage of his hometown of Mystic and was glad people had moved beyond the slaughter of whales for oil. But now he considered the irony of his life at sea on an oil platform, producing oil and sometimes polluting the sea when spills occurred. He pondered this and felt a sense of sorrow that humans had not learned a harmonious existence with the sea as had the dolphins. He could sense Peek's curiosity at his internal philosophizing. Then Jonas asked, "But why were you gone so long?"

"You mustn't rush things, time does that all by itself. I was hunting. The humpbacks found a huge school of fish, and we fed for three suns—three days, as you say—until we were full and strong. Then I explored along the coast where many interesting things can be found. There are many wrecked ships along this coast, you know, and I often search out crayfish and langoustines in those areas. Did you know it can be quite tricky catching such animals? I also played at the seal colony for a day. Seals will do anything for fun."

"I've been reading, trying to understand how it is we can talk to each other," Jonas said.

"We just do, because we are of the same origins. That's why." Peek understood intuitively that reading for Jonas was like watching things intently for himself.

"Do you know how the Greeks think dolphins came into being?" Jonas asked.

"No. Not only that, but I don't know of these Greeks."

"Well, they were a group of humans that sort of started civilization, founders of a lot of basic philosophy and early science. The Greeks said that dolphins are of such temperament because of the debt they owe to Poseidon."

"And who might Poseidon be?" Peek asked. He was amused by these human myths.

"He's the god of the sea, at least according to the Greeks," Jonas said. "I've recently received a letter from my sister. She is a teacher, and she is intent on educating me on the mythology of humans, gods, and dolphins."

"A sister?"

"Yes, a sister is a member of a human family, from the same parents. You must have sisters and brothers."

"Maybe. I do have offspring. I swim with them and show them the many joys and dangers of the ocean. Do you have offspring?"

"Me? Oh, no. I don't think that will happen. One needs a wife for that."

"A mate. Yes, that is necessary," Peek said, and whistled as if laughing. "So who is this Greek you talk about? Maybe he can help you."

"Poseidon? No. I think not. The Greeks called him the god of the sea, as I said."

"Ah, whales," Peek said.

"I guess that could be one way of looking at it," Jonas said. "Anyway, it seems that Dionysus—the god of wine, which is something humans drink that makes them lose their senses—was to be sold as a slave by the crew of a boat he had hired. Dionysus, being a god, used his powers to his advantage. He transformed the boat's oars into serpents, filled the air with the sound of flutes, and filled the vessel with vines that sprouted from his loins. This so scared the seamen that they leapt from the ship rather than face Dionysus."

"I've watched many things happening on many ships, but I've never seen that!" Peek said.

"Nor I."

"And I would not like to!" Peek slapped the water with a flipper to urge Jonas to continue; he was rather enjoying the tale.

Jonas grinned, and then said, "Well, as the story goes, Poseidon watched this series of events and in his great benevolence granted the sailors clemency from a drowning at sea."

"Ah, a good god, then," Peek said, "He must have been a whale! I think I like this Poseidon."

"Yes, a good god by all rights," Jonas said. "So by saving these men they were transformed into dolphins. Because of this they are forever grateful to Poseidon and promise to always do his bidding. Poseidon's request was one of kindness and compassion, and that is what we find in dolphins to this day."

"I don't think I believe it—I mean that dolphins come from man. Maybe the other way around, though," Peek said. "Besides not all dolphins are kind and compassionate."

"I suspect not," Jonas said, "but I'm sure they are more so than humans. We have so much fighting and wars and social injustice."

"There is some of that between home families, too, but we generally work things out or swim to another part of the ocean."

"We humans can't always go elsewhere. There are too many of us. So you don't believe my little story?"

"We dolphins have other ideas about all this."

"Please tell me," Jonas said.

"When I was young I lived in a warmer sea far from here into the morning sun."

"To the east? How far—how far of a swim?" Jonas asked.

"Many, many months. But I swam it when I was young to escape recapture. I swam and swam, for I was so afraid. You see, I was captured when I had only been with my mother for a season. I never saw her again."

"This is terrible. Were you near Australia? That's a land mass on the other side of the next ocean over."

"That could be. When I was in captivity, humans often came into the Pool—a terrible, stark place they kept us dolphins. One of the humans was pregnant. We could all tell because of the small being within."

"How could you tell that?" Jonas asked.

"We let out noise, and it comes back to us as shapes. I see you with my eyes, but I also see you throughout because of my soundings—my second eyes. I hear what you look like. I sound you."

"Sonar, of course. So you hear the echo of the shape of what is in people, and you could therefore see the fetus of this pregnant woman—like ultrasound."

"Sound, yes. I noticed that the baby within was shaped much differently than the human without. The unborn baby had a tail. I also know what my children looked like before they were born, because I had sounded them. They have a tail but keep it after birth. The unborn baby of the human and the unborn baby of us dolphins look similar. I think it is sad that humans lose their tails."

"We call that relationship *evolution*—all mammals are related but have adapted differently to different environments."

"That *is* so," Peek said. "Because I believe we dolphins have always been at sea, while you humans were born from us and are the relatives we've sent onto land to look around. But for some reason they never came back to the sea. So what do you think of my idea?"

"Pretty interesting. I was also reading that some humans think dolphins originated in the water, then adapted to the land, but then returned to the water for some evolutionary reason."

"It is obvious, Jonas, the oceans are the place to be. One is never thirsty, like the land creatures we can see along the sandy coast. One never gets too hot, except when we get stuck on the beach. The ocean is a better place, by our way of thinking."

"I can see why. That's probably why I've chosen to dive and live on and in the ocean most of my life. I do love it so."

"I know, Jonas, I know. That is another reason I came to find you."

CHAPTER

6

Sleeping, sleeping, youth is past.
Namibian proverb

The western coast of Namibia is a harsh land. The rugged shores are dotted with the bleached skeletons of ships that have run aground during the fierce southern gales and the brutal northwesterly storms. Because of this it is called the Skeleton Coast.

Thousand-foot-high sand dunes are the backdrop to this coast. Sand ripples mimic the waves and are moved by the same winds that stir up the ocean. Rivers that start far inland are dusty valleys by the time they reach the sea. Some flow only once a decade, and others have not held water within human memory.

It is windy year round, and the force blows sand from the beaches inland into the Namib Desert. The furtive Orange River winds its way reluctantly to the ocean, a poor reflection of its once grander self when, during the wetter times of the dinosaurs, it flowed strong and wild. The river brought diamonds to the sea, weathering the vast kimberlite fields from the interior of South Africa. The river and the ocean currents spread the gems for a thousand miles along the South African and Namibian coasts. It was into that harsh land that Bebe February had been born fifty years earlier. People from his tribe had been conscripted with virtually no pay to sweep diamonds from bedrock cracks for their South African diamond masters.

"It is a stark view, even from here, don't you think?" Bebe asked.

45

"Very," Jonas said. The two men leaned against a steel railing on the drill deck of the *Atlantic Stroom*. It had been another long day's work. Jonas had spent three hours underwater and four hours in decompression after a rigorous work period effecting repairs on the lower part of the starboard pontoon. He was exhausted and needed to smell fresh air, not the bottled stuff he'd been living on most of the day.

"I'm sure I've told you that my father used to work in the diamond mines along the coast. And me as well, when I was so much younger," Bebe said.

"Yes, but not in detail. It is a painful thing for you to remember, I think."

"Yes. But as I watch you and that dolphin, I find I am reassessing my life. What are these relationships? They are so fleeting sometimes. I miss my father. Your father, he was a fisherman, I recall," Bebe asked.

"Yes, back in Mystic, Connecticut."

"It is no wonder you ended up on the sea."

Jonas spied a small boat five or six kilometers north of the *Atlantic Stroom*. It caught his eye, and now he pointed it out to Bebe. "Take a look at that boat. I wonder if they know what they're doing."

"Ah, just Lüderitz fishermen, or maybe seafloor diamond dredgers," Bebe said. He returned to their topic of conversation but, like Jonas, kept an eye on the boat. "Well, Jonas, this dolphin of yours seems to be putting you in a contemplative mood these days."

"You know, I've been doing repairs and fittings since I was fifteen, welding in a small boatyard in Mystic. Mostly on small fishing boats. I learned seamanship from my father and some of the older men. Sometimes I'd go out to sea and help my dad, but he liked the fact that I was learning another trade. I think he foresaw the decline of fishing in the North Atlantic," Jonas said.

He studied the small boat as it set a course that would bring it between the *Atlantic Stroom* and the rocky reef along the Skeleton Coast. "You know, my dad said I'd better be prepared to get out of there when the fishing industry changed. He said to me that one morning he woke up and realized he was old—his youthfulness had just vanished. That scared the hell out of me. I remember those days so well."

"Yes, not knowing the future is both reality and a fear," Bebe said. He eyed the approaching boat as well. "Huh. I wonder if they are in trouble?"

"Doesn't look like it yet," Jonas said, following Bebe's gaze toward the small craft. "But they will be if they get too close to that reef."

"So that's when you went to sea?" Bebe asked. "When your dad had that realization?"

"Well, it led to that. It was a stormy time in the family. With the layoffs, none of us saw any future. My dad wasn't the only one feeling old. Some of my friends went to New York to look for jobs, but nothing much came of it. I stayed in Mystic. Maddy was teaching school. The rest is history, as they say, you know. I took an industrial diving course and began using my welding experience and general knowledge of machines underwater. I loved it, so I stayed with it."

"And now here we are, a decade later, living on this steel island!" Bebe said.

"Yup. At least my sister and I are still close. Being the teacher that she is, she's always sending me stuff—trying to broaden my literary horizons, as she puts it. I send her notes from the sea."

"Did you tell her about your dolphin friend?" Bebe asked.

"Yeah. I think she thinks I'm off my rocker, and I think what she's thinking might not be too far from the truth!"

"Ha! Any man who spends as much time in the water as you is crazy. Dead right!" Bebe said and then laughed heartily.

"I think that boat is making for shore," Jonas said, interrupting the light moment. "If they aren't, they'd better put out an anchor soon."

"Not on that coast," Bebe said. "That's the diamond coast, as you know. They'll suffer on that shore. There are no good things there. My father died in the diamond mines there. It was a long time ago, but I don't think much has changed."

Jonas looked at his old friend. He didn't often open up like this. "You okay?"

"Dead right. Just remembering."

"I must say, you becoming a meteorologist is a far and welcome cry from a fate as a diamond digger."

"What I tell you, my friend, is only known to my family. I have told no one, so hold this close. Perhaps it matters no more. But my father died so I could live." Bebe paused and seemed to scowl at the coast, his eyes fixed on the small boat as it made way, as if the boat's actions had triggered a deep memory.

Jonas studied the profile of his friend. He realized there were secrets in this man he would never know, never understand. Bebe had bridged the gap between childhood in a subsistence village without electricity or medical facilities to become a scientist on a highly technical drilling platform. Jonas stood in awe of the man.

"My father wanted more for me, not necessarily a better education or a career in science, but he wanted me—his only son—to get out. But it is not cheap to do this." Bebe paused. Then he continued in a quiet voice, "So we devised a plan. We took back some of the diamonds we had been digging for the Company—the master of the diamond cartel. After all, the diamonds came from the land we lived on, our tribal lands. We were owed that much because of the paltry salary, and because we were treated like animals—I will never forget the humiliating body searches.

So one of my uncles said if that is what they see us as, then we will fulfill their own prophecy and take our diamonds back."

"So you stole diamonds from the Company!" Jonas said. He had never been to a diamond mine, but he had looked at the coastal operations through binoculars from his vantage point on the *Atlantic Stroom*. He looked toward the coast where pyramids of sand—enormous spoil piles from the coastal mines—could clearly be seen.

"Yes, we did. We would tuck them into our bodies or wrap them in cloths and throw them over the fences or swallow them. Dozens of us did this, and we started accumulating diamonds outside the compound. Our relatives from the villages would collect them under cover of darkness and bury the hoard where the Company could not find them. But one day the Company caught my father. He had swallowed a number of stones, and they showed up on an X-ray. You see, the Company would randomly pick some of us out to be X-rayed. We knew there was this risk and that some of us would be caught, but the agreement was that those who remained free would watch after the families of those men who were caught."

"What did they do?"

"One particular guard was a hateful and cruel man and had no more patience for the likes of us. He killed my father in front of us all. He cut him open." Bebe paused. "The diamonds he had swallowed glinted in his blood on the hot dry sand."

"My god, Bebe." Jonas could say nothing else. The two men stood there at the rail for long moments in silence.

"My friends held me back, or else I would have killed that guard—and be killed as well. In the commotion that followed I left the compound with several others. We retrieved our share of the diamonds we had already taken, and I fled to Angola. There I sold them and continued north. I spent several years in West Africa—in Ghana—before I decided to go to Europe. I had learned much about the Europeans while in West Africa, and the money I had was of such quantity that I could well afford to travel there. I ended up in London and after a time became involved with a circle of educated friends. With their help I was accepted at university. The rest, as you say, is history."

Jonas could say nothing. He just placed a hand on Bebe's shoulder, and the two men passed the moment in silence.

Suddenly there was a loud boom. The two men looked up, and there on the water a black cloud of smoke issued from the small fishing boat they had noticed earlier.

"Bebe, sound the alarm! That boat will crash to bits on the reef if we can't get there to save them! Meet me at the starboard lifeboat. I'll get it ready."

Bebe ran to one of the muster points. He slammed his fist into the large red alarm button, and the klaxon blared into the calm afternoon air. Bebe then picked up the phone and called the bridge to let the captain know there was a boat in distress, that the alarm was not for some problem on the *Atlantic Stroom*. This task done, he bolted to the starboard rail to join Jonas.

At the starboard lifeboat station, the evacuation lifeboats were stored in chutes for rapid deployment. Jonas called to one of the crew as Bebe joined them. In their practiced emergency response protocol, Bebe, Jonas, and the other crew member hopped into one of the fully enclosed boats, strapped themselves in, checked engine systems, and—thanks to Bebe's communication with the bridge—received permission to launch, all in under two minutes.

The crewman sat at the helm—assuming the job of the boat's pilot. He yelled back to Bebe and Jonas, "Ready—we are green to go."

Bebe and Jonas responded with a "Go!" The pilot punched the release mechanisms. The lifeboat—like an escape capsule—shot down the chute as a rapid-release cable pulled it into action. The loud grating sound of the hull on the chute was deafening and then suddenly silent. It was a fifteen-meter drop to the sea once the boat cleared the chute. For a moment the feeling of weightlessness enveloped Jonas, Bebe, and the pilot. Then came the impact with the sea. The boat's torpedo-like hull pierced the sea and slammed the three men into their harnesses. Momentarily submerged, the boat rocked and rolled, then popped up to the surface like a cork. Seawater drained from the covered deck, and rivulets of it streamed down the windows.

From the *Atlantic Stroom* the emergency response officer radioed to the lifeboat. The tinny sounding voice said, "We have people in the water. Your estimated distance is two kilometers. The boat is breaking up fast."

It took a moment for Jonas to collect himself from the rapid series of events. Their pilot fired up the twin diesel engines and was steering toward the coast. Jonas joined Bebe at the rear bulkhead and undogged the hatch. They clamored onto the narrow deck to look for the distressed ship.

"There, see it?" Bebe yelled.

"Yes, it is definitely going down fast. Must have been an engine explosion," Jonas said. The pilot gunned the engine to its twenty-five kilometers per hour maximum—redlined—and motored toward the disaster.

Jonas glanced at his watch. Time was racing by, the water was cold, and the shoreline treacherous. Already five minutes had elapsed since the explosion. He could see people in the water, and only about a third of the small boat was visible above the low swell. He could hear the breakers on the rocky reef as the swell met bottom and reared up into frothing waves. They were still seven minutes out, and that didn't even begin to cover the time needed to pull people from the sea.

Bebe glanced at Jonas. "I don't think we'll be in time. I can make out at least ten people."

Just then a second explosion rocked the wreck and sent fragments of wood and steel laced with flame, black smoke, and steam high into the air. Now the entire crew of the small boat was in the water, and orange life preservers could be seen around the bobbing heads.

"Five minutes out," the pilot yelled. The bow of the lifeboat rose above its wake as it raced through the water.

"There!" Bebe yelled, pointing to the frothing water between the lifeboat and the wreck.

"Dolphins!" Jonas said. He could see six . . . no, ten . . . no, fifteen or more dolphins racing toward the wreck at twice the speed of the lifeboat. He stood in awe and amazement at the scene.

"What the heck is that!" came the cry from the pilot. He could see fins and turbulent water through the water-smeared window from his pilot's seat as the boat bounced along. "Sharks?"

Bebe poked his head into the cabin and yelled above the roar of the engines. "No man, it is the dolphins!"

"No friggin' way, you kiddin' me?"

"Dead right!" yelled Bebe, and rejoined Jonas topside.

On the deck of the *Atlantic Stroom*, crew members lined up along the rail to watch the action. Many had binoculars, and a few even had cameras with telephoto lenses.

Minutes passed.

Jonas and Bebe watched as the shoal of dolphins swam into the men bobbing in their life vests. He could see, now that they were less than a half kilometer away, that some were panicking—perhaps thinking the fins were those of sharks. But they soon realized that dolphins were among them. Jonas could see one man reach for the dorsal fin of one of the dolphins.

"Jonas, look at that! Just look at that." Bebe leaned as far forward as he could on the deck, as if willing the lifeboat forward. "It is a miracle, dead right."

The other men followed the example of the man hanging onto the dolphin, and soon they were all taken in tow by the dolphins.

"What the . . ." the pilot yelled up to Jonas.

"All engines stop!" Jonas yelled. He could not believe his eyes. The dolphins were bringing the stranded crew to the lifeboat, away from the hazard of the reef. As the engines were cut and the lifeboat slowed and settled into the water, the first dolphin brought one of the survivors alongside.

Bebe and Jonas reached down, grabbed the hands of the waterlogged man, and pulled him aboard. Then another, and then another.

The victims were Portuguese fishermen, and many were crossing themselves and uttering prayers. Each helped the next, and soon twelve men in orange life vests sat on the top deck of the lifeboat. Four fishermen had been lost to the explosions. The men slumped on deck. Some had burns, others bruises and cuts. But they were alive.

All at once a dolphin leaped from the water.

"Ha! You are a miracle," cried Jonas as he recognized his friend Peek.

"You that dolphin know?" asked one of the shivering fishermen in broken English. His wide eyes were set in a lined, sun-leathered face above a curly beard.

"Yes," Jonas said. "Yes, I do."

News of the remarkable rescue hit the wires and became a sensation around the world. Although distant and a bit blurred, photographs from the *Atlantic Stroom* crew confirmed that more than a dozen dolphins had helped the fishermen away from their stricken boat and to safety. One of the photos showed Bebe and Jonas as they pulled the ragtag survivors aboard the *Atlantic Stroom*'s lifeboat. That made the front page of the *Cape Times*, *Le Monde*, *Die Welt*, the *London Times*, *El País*, and, of course, *The New York Times*.

Following the international blitz of positive news revolving around the *Atlantic Stroom*'s brave crew and its spectacular association with what one paper called "the lifeguard dolphins," Jonas received another note from Cape Town:

Mr. James,

You have brought remarkable good fortune and press to our often besieged petroleum company. We, here in the Cape Town head office, would like to express our gratitude for your service, and for the quick, clearheaded rescue efforts of those unfortunate Portuguese fishermen by you and your fellow crewmen Bebe February and helmsman pilot Richards. Your efforts were above and beyond your normal duties. That being said, we are again impressed with your unusual association with sea creatures, the first being the close call with the shark, and now this unparalleled display of the so dubbed lifeguard dolphins. Please anticipate a bonus in your monthly check. Keep up the good work.

My best regards,
Johan Van Stuer
General Manager
Cape Town Operations

Jonas had made his way up to the weather room and discovered Bebe, as well as the helmsman, had received the same letter, except Jonas's was embellished with the comment about his association with sea creatures. Bebe was all smiles, fueled in part by the news of a bonus.

Madeleine stood outside Bartleby's coffee shop on West Main Street in downtown Mystic. She stared at *The New York Times* front page on the newsstand. That was her brother. On the front page. With dolphins. The headline read:

DOLPHINS, OIL DRILLING DIVER, NAMIBIAN WEATHERMAN TEAM UP TO SAVE FISHERMEN

The story began: "Johan Van Stuer, General Manager of Cape Town Operations, is proud of his men and his dolphins..." Madeleine popped fifty cents into the dispenser and pulled out a paper. She stood there and read the entire article. The story was astonishing. It was unbelievable! It was her brother!

The world spun just a little bit, and her tether to reality slipped a notch.

CHAPTER

7

Sweet taste is never longer than your finger.
Namibian proverb

A new calf had been born recently within Peek's home family. The calf came into its aquatic world tail first and open-eyed. Its mother rapidly nudged the young one to the surface for its first breath of air. Elation and joy rippled through the home family. The cycle of life would continue, and the love of the ocean passed on.

A dolphin is so much a part of the ocean! Fundamental elements, such as sodium and potassium and chloride, are present in its blood in the same proportions as those found in seawater. The newly arrived calf would now swim just above its mother in front of her dorsal fin. This is where school was held—constantly watching the motions of its mother, what she ate, how she interacted with others, what to do to stay clear of danger. Body contact is constant. The mother whistles almost continuously for days after the baby's birth so that the new one learns her voice. The next five to six years would find the mother and young dolphin together constantly.

In Peek's home family there were five to ten births each year. But by the end of the first year some of these young will not have survived. The ocean is a harsh place. What with Old Death lurking about, and the orcas, and the humans, and the occasional intense storms, there were plenty of dangers. Because of this the dolphins had learned to live for the day. An uncontainable love of life, a lust for life, spurred them on. Their intense curiosity and long memories and deep love for one another resulted in a highly developed social group. It was flexible and fair, and they were very much dependent upon one another.

As the young dolphins grew, the young males might leave the home family to form their own smaller transient groups. These transient males swam far and wide, sometimes returning to protect the home family or help with hunting, and of course they returned for mating. These dolphins were welcomed back, and they brought with them their experiences, to the benefit of the home family. Then they sometimes gathered others and ventured off to form a new home family, perhaps on another part of the coast they had discovered that suited them. But the home families mingled periodically, thereby enriching the group with new offspring and experiences. There were also challenges for mates, and some of the older dolphins had rake-like scars from the teeth of other dolphins, inflicted on one another during disputes and confrontations for dominance.

Transient males swam for days and weeks along the southwestern coast of Africa. Peek sometimes joined them—as a friend and teacher to many, and a father and grandfather to some. They swam as sleek arrows, traveling up to thirty-five kilometers an hour in the vast ocean, covering hundreds of kilometers, sounding the area for fish and exploring the bays and reefs.

The amazing speed of dolphins is augmented by their unique surface. Their skin moves in a rippling motion, reacting to subtle changes in pressure as the water streams across their bodies. The substantial layer of blubber under their skin is not attached to any muscle, but rather to a system of ridges to reduce drag. As a result, they are swift and gleaming creatures. Their skin also secretes small amounts of oil, which keep it moist and pliable in its constant bath of seawater. Sometimes, after a dolphin launches itself from the water and then dives back in, a small oily ring from its skin is left on the surface.

When the transient dolphins discover a school of fish, then comes a noisy and lively time. The dolphins swim in ever decreasing circles while diving beneath the increasingly confused fish. This clever motion, similar to the method whales use to hunt, drives the fish toward the surface, and soon the sea is a froth of fish and dolphins. The dolphins can even stun the smaller fish with intense acoustic blasts. Hunting is a cacophony of activity.

Peek had been exploring with a dozen of the young males for several days. Spray, one of the maturing dolphins in the ad hoc shoal was a close companion of Peek's, and he was developing a keen sense of the ocean and all that lived in it and upon it.

"The ships of the humans come from the north again, many of them. I heard the noise," Spray chirped as he swam strong and confident alongside Peek, conveying his anxiety to his friend. The propeller noises stress the dolphins and interrupt their high-frequency communications.

Even though Peek also disliked the ships, he had a greater kindness within, which had drawn him and the others to save the fishermen from their sinking boat and the relentless waves of the reef. It was an internal conflict he did not fully understand, but he understood the preciousness of life.

The boats that Spray had heard were part of a large Portuguese fleet that periodically fished the southern shelf. Many of the fishing boats often overstepped into Namibian territorial waters, and eight of them had been confiscated. They sat rotting in Luderitz Harbor until the astronomical fines had been paid. These boats, however, were like sharks within a reef as far as the dolphins were concerned: they could come out at any moment and lay their nets.

"Yes, we will stay south of them for a while," Peek said.

The two swam together for some time. Peek had much on his mind and wished to discuss it with his human friend. He was unsure, however, how his dolphin friend would react if he knew of the meetings with a human. Spray sensed Peek's need to talk.

"So what is on your mind, my teacher?"

"Hmmm, so very much. Strange things are happening these days in the ocean."

"More and more humans, fewer and fewer fish. And Old Death ever lurking," Spray said. "I heard you have been swimming near the steel island recently. What draws you there?"

"Has it been that obvious?"

"Well, some of us have noticed. You know, you have many admirers, and some of them follow you around like parasite fish. Even if they can't always keep up with you, they still know where you have been. So what is there, my teacher?"

"What I tell you will not make sense. I have been communicating with a human."

"What! That's foolish! Are you sounding nothing but bubbles? Have the burrow worms got to your brain?" Spray was astonished.

"I wondered. But this human is a good one, not like those who captured me or the ones who maim our home family. Even the ones we pull from the sea do not understand us. But this one on the steel island, well, I was somehow drawn to him."

"And what does this human say?"

"He is as surprised as me that we can communicate. I have heard of this before—I recall my mother telling me about it. But other than that there are only rumors, mythical tales. No one I've asked recalls any real or productive interaction. I am wary, but my curiosity is overwhelming. So I return, and we talk."

"What about?" Spray asked, his own curiosity intensifying. He might like to meet this human, having never actually seen one up close.

"Of many things. Of the ocean and why humans occupy it. Of our possible relationships in time, of our origins and attitudes. Of all things," Peek said, his voice resonating with amazement at how much he enjoyed talking to Jonas Jeremy James—the human who seemed to love the ocean as he did.

Jonas had been diving again. This time he had taken a small, one-man submersible down on a tether to the wellhead which sat on the ocean floor at a depth of 435 meters. The convenient aspect of the submersible was that he would not have to decompress on arriving at the surface, due to the pressurized environment maintained in the sub. Jonas thought of Peek and the fact that dolphins could easily dive rather deep quite naturally—300 to 500 meters, with their lungs full of sacks of air to keep everything from collapsing. The diving dolphin allows its musculature to compress, causing it to sink like a rock. In this way the dolphin does not waste precious oxygen required for brain and organ functions on muscle movement. Once at depth, the dolphin has enough oxygen to use its muscles to shoot back to the surface with its powerful fluke. It can stay down for seven to eight minutes. Jonas thought of these things every time he entered the water.

Jonas's tasks on this dive were mechanical. He performed a visual and acoustic routine maintenance and inspection. He was looking for leaks and undue corrosion around the wellhead and blowout preventer. He had a new purpose now, having met Peek, to keep the ocean cleaner. He conducted his inspection with floodlights and video cameras, now and then testing a valve or a join with the two mechanical arms on the submersible. The servo mechanisms whined in response as Jonas pushed the joysticks this way and that. The thruster on the submersible now and then kicked up the fine silt that covered the seafloor, sending up clouds of murk through which no light could penetrate. Care was therefore taken to minimize disturbing the bottom muds. In the flat light the occasional shrimp or crayfish would skitter by, and now and then a bottom-dwelling fish would swim into view.

With $200 million of high-tech equipment on the bottom, there was lots of this type of work to do. The oil company was about to begin installing a floating dock, which would allow tankers to load up with crude oil ten kilometers out to sea. The drill platform—stationary like an island—would act as a temporary service and maintenance station to assist with construction of the floating docks and pumping stations, as well as the pumping of the crude oil. Up to this point the *Atlantic Stroom* had been just an exploration platform, drilling multiple holes to discover the location and extent of the submarine oil resources. Now, with the discovery confirmed, tankers would be brought in to transport the oil to distant refineries. The *Atlantic Stroom* would help make the transition from an exploration platform to a production facility. Then the semi could be moved off site to continue exploration elsewhere along the continental shelf. Bebe and Jonas and many of the other crew would move to a new oil field, just as they had many times before.

Once the new wellhead and pump array infrastructure was in place, the crude oil would be drawn from its geologic vault beneath the seafloor up to the waiting tankers. It was a very efficient way to transfer crude oil, and it also created a buffer zone of ten kilometers of ocean between the pumping station and the coast should a spill occur. The oil company would then have time, providing a storm was not in progress, to begin containment and clean up after a spill. It all looked perfect in the plans. But there had been many oil spills, not only along this coast but in all of the world's oceans. The ecological impact to the oceans, the coast, and estuaries had been great.

Jonas wondered if there might not be a better way to run human civilization than by burning oil pumped from the sea-floor. The ocean was too precious to ruin, a natural resource in its own right. It was a living and breathing ecosystem that could not tolerate the more destructive human activities indefinitely. He knew that everything from fewer fish, to chemical and petro-leum pollution, to garbage washed from the land—even increas-ingly alarming amounts of very small beads of plastic—were the effects of our impact on the oceans, causing the death of many species. He had felt Peek's sadness about all of this, even if the dolphin hadn't understood the scientific details.

After several hours on the bottom he radioed up to the sur-face that all looked fine and flooded his ballast tanks with com-pressed air. The submersible sluggishly responded and began the slow ascent. Jonas kept the tether attached to the cable systems running from the wellhead on the bottom to the semi above him so he wouldn't drift down current into open ocean. There was a strong three-knot bottom current, which the submersible's thrusters could barely manage. So care had to be taken.

Viewing the ocean from the perspective of the small thick window of the mini submarine impressed upon Jonas that the vastness seen at its surface was surpassed by the vastness of its depths.

At a depth of twenty meters the ocean is still a dark place, although the faintest light can sometimes be seen if the water is clear—a situation that is rare off the coast of Namibia. At ten meters visibility is better; on a good day you can see through several meters of water. It was at this depth that Jonas saw Peek flash by the porthole of the submersible. He immediately felt elation. Then a second dolphin swam by, pausing momentarily to look in at Jonas.

"That's the human?" Spray chirped to Peek.

"Yes, that's the one."

"I thought you said he swam. Looks to me like he's in a sinking ship. How can you talk to him in that thing?"

"He usually swims," Peek said. "I've seen him in this thing before when he wants to go deep. It's sort of a ship, but it doesn't just sink. It floats up, like it's doing now. He'll get out when it reaches the air."

"Humph," grunted Spray as he paused again to look in the porthole. He could see Jonas's face peering out at him. "Looks like any other human to me."

The two dolphins followed the submersible up to the surface but kept their distance as it was hauled out of the water. To the dolphins, it looked like a great yellow misshapen whale off of which they sounded only hard reflections and a varied pandemonium of electronic noises.

Bebe February, who was observing the recovery of the submersible by Willy and Piet, smiled broadly when he saw the dolphins break the surface. As the hatch opened and Jonas stuck his head out, Bebe yelled down from the weather deck, "Hey my friend, your good luck companion is back and has brought a friend!"

The other crew members all laughed and joked with Jonas about the dolphins. Some had taken to calling Jonas "the dolphinman," and they kidded him that he had fins under his jacket. They were all more or less aware of the odd relationship developing between Jonas and the one dolphin ever since the shark attack, and even more so after the rescue of the fishermen. But the crew, as do many at sea, paid some deference to superstition and considered the dolphin's presence good luck. There was a noticeable decline in morale if the dolphin was not seen for a few days. When faced with tasks and chores, some of the crew had taken to saying, "By the dolphin, we'll get this done!" Subconsciously everyone treated Jonas with more consideration and respect these days. He was good luck, and that was always needed at sea.

Jonas laughed along with his mates at their waggery but was cautious not to attempt communication with Peek while others were about. That part was not known to the crew, except possibly Bebe. Peek seemed to understand this, and the two dolphins slapped the water with their flukes and vanished in the fathomless ocean.

The crew let out a cheer, taking that—and anything the dolphins did—as a sign of good fortune.

These were good times, and the weeks passed with frequent visits from Peek. He and Jonas no longer needed to be physically touching to communicate, just in close proximity. Their mental powers were developing to new and unexpected levels. Jonas learned of the ocean as Peek learned of humankind.

CHAPTER

8

New things lie in front of those who move.
Namibian proverb

Madeleine sat in Bartleby's coffee shop, across from the Bank Square bookstore, with her best friend, Mary Beth. She loved this small community and how everything seemed to be connected to the Mystic River or the ocean. The water was a tangible presence to everyone who lived here—a touchstone, of sorts, that grounded people. The sea was as emotional as any person in its many moods from calm to fury. The blare of the signals from the historic drawbridge reminded her that there was always someone going somewhere on the Mystic River. But now she was lost in thought about her brother and uncharacteristically silent. Mary Beth began to worry.

"Are you all right?" she asked.

"Oh," Madeleine whispered, her voice quivering slightly as tears clouded her eyes. "I don't know. Jonas's letters are so strange. He keeps writing about this dolphin and how he's talking to it. And then there was that *New York Times* front page. Who would have thought he would make the news? But he writes that he's talking to a dolphin. No, Mary B, I am not all right."

"Talking to a dolphin?" Mary Beth raised her eyebrows in disbelief, but tried to control her surprise. "I thought Jonas was on a drill platform, not some aquarium."

"He is. He's a diver, he does welding, he fixes things underwater. No, this is some fish . . ." Madeleine paused and rolled her eyes. "I mean a *mammal*, as he keeps reminding me in his letters, that he *met* while diving."

"That's pretty weird, Maddy." Mary Beth took a sip of tea and frowned. She put the cup down and folded her hands on the table. Her round face was framed by close-cropped blond hair, and her expression was serious as she studied her friend. "What are you going to do?"

"I don't know. Should I go down there and see him?" Madeleine looked up, hungry for advice.

Mary Beth shrugged. "Maybe. Fall break is coming up, so you've got vacation time. But can you go and visit him on this drill rig he's on? Do they allow that sort of thing?"

"I don't know. I don't care," Madeleine said, looking up and smiling at how she must sound. Talking to Mary Beth always made her feel better. "You know, I went to the Mystic Aquarium last weekend and started learning about these dolphins. The marine biologists there are amazing. They rescue sea animals and help them back to health. It's like a refuge, but one where you can learn and be part of the ocean without knowing how to dive. I learned there's all sorts of dolphins. They're pretty smart, at least according to the guy I talked to. They hum and sing. They study objects that the researchers put in front of them and seem to admire certain things. They have a brain as big as ours, you know."

Mary Beth shook her head. She hadn't known that about dolphins, but she was intrigued by her friend's enthusiasm.

"I asked him—this marine biologist—who by the way was pretty cute," Madeleine said, smiling down at the tabletop. "I asked him if a person could communicate with a dolphin. He said it was possible and that a lot of research had been done on it. He said that dolphins talk with a series of clicks and squeaks and whistles, and they *hear* all these noises through their lower jaw. He called it an acoustic window, sort of like our ears. They make all these sounds from this fatty organ in their forehead, he called that a melon."

"Weird," Mary Beth said. "Can you imagine us talking that way?"

"No, that's my problem. Jonas keeps writing me that he's talking to this dolphin. So is he crazy, or what? How could he understand all those noises they make? The guy played a tape of dolphin talk, and it sounded pretty strange to me, but it's kind of beautiful. I had never seen one. They have dolphins there only when they need rescuing, and they release them when they're healthy again. But I watched a lot of video the marine biologist had taken during his research. When they look at you straight on, they seem to have a smile—but I couldn't tell what was behind the dolphin's smile. Mary B, they're so beautiful. I can see why Jonas is captivated by them. But I don't understand why he thinks he's talking to them."

"I've seen dolphins," Mary Beth said. "When I lived in California, we used to go to Marine World and watch them jump through the hoops and fetch things in the water. They sure seemed smart to me."

"I know what you mean. But Jonas said that a lot of the captive dolphins have a sense of sadness."

"Maybe that's what Jonas means, just that he can sense them a little bit."

"I definitely got the feeling he thinks we shouldn't pen them up like cows," Madeleine said. "I found a quote from Jacques Cousteau in a book I was reading." Madeleine pulled a scrap of paper out of her purse. "Here, I wrote it down. Let's see. He said, *No sooner does man discover intelligence than he tries to involve it in his own stupidity.* The guy at the aquarium told me that all sorts of experiments have been done on dolphins—it was pretty terrible. So after I read that quote I kept wondering if Jonas had discovered something, realized something down there where he's working off the African coast. Something new and different."

"What do you mean he *realized* something?" Mary Beth asked. She was becoming even more intrigued. It was clear to her that Madeleine was taking this situation very seriously.

"I don't know, I just don't know."

"Sounds to me like you really want to go down and see Jonas. I think you should."

"Do you? You don't think I'm crazy?"

"Well, I don't think *you're* crazy—maybe your brother is, though." Mary Beth laughed to try to lighten the mood. "But you should go, and maybe I should go with you!"

CHAPTER

9

If your mother has not taught you,
life will teach you.
Namibian proverb

The young dolphin named Dart heard a noise—a strange new sound—and started for it. Trusting and curious, not wise or cautious, the sound tickled his senses and gnawed at his imagination. It was a perfect day to explore. The home family members were busy chasing down cuttlefish; Dart had had his fill by catching the pieces that littered the water from the feeding frenzy of the larger dolphins. He shot toward the surface and leapt in the waves.

Bright, the young dolphin's mother, soon noticed her one-year-old son missing from the home family. A young dolphin is fast and impetuous, and she had seen Dart wander off before. She emitted her distinctive whistle, but there was no response. Again she whistled, and the other females in the shoal quickly chirped in recognition that one of the young had strayed while the noise was in the water. Bright kept whistling as she swam rapidly in wider and wider circles, finally breaking away from the shoal. It was there that the full impact of the noise assaulted her senses. It was much closer than she had thought. Bright was near panic as she realized her son must be following it. The other females gave chase, whistling and chirping warnings in the hope that Dart would heed their pleas and return to the shoal.

Peek immediately realized what was happening. The noise was distant and ominous to him, but the ruckus from the females was urgent. He could tell that fifteen of them had stayed behind, herding the other youngsters in a circle so that their curiosity wouldn't overwhelm their own mothers' warnings. It was hard to contain the shoal; as the noise increased, it interfered with the dolphins' natural high-frequency communications. Peek raced madly toward Bright, for he knew she must be homing in on her son, and her son was his son.

Dart did not hear his mother. The young dolphin was focused on a huge school of herring ahead. Even with his limited experience he could sense that there was something wrong. The herring were gathering together in an unusually tight school, and many were breaching and splashing at the ocean's surface. Yet Dart could not detect any whales or dolphins circling the fish, a hunting technique he had recently learned. The strange sound was much louder and started to assault his senses. He became nervous and he slowed down, but he continued toward the massive school of fish. Thoughts raced through his mind: *Where is my mother? Will she know what this noise is that fills the water and hurts my head? Why are there so many fish here and none of the other dolphins?* The ocean was thrumming with sound—the rasping of fish against fish, their splashing at the surface, the ominous groan of the noise which had first attracted Dart, and then a faint but urgent whistle.

Bright sped through the water trying to locate her son. She continued whistling in the hopes that the emotion it could trigger in the young dolphin would overwhelm his curiosity and make him turn back. Bright was suddenly aware of a strong dolphin swimming alongside. It was Peek. Peek the wise one. Peek the fast. Peek who knew the ways of man. Bright and Peek communicated quickly with rapid chirps, body language, and subtle layers of telepathy. Their love and devotion to each other flowed freely, and Bright felt a moment of comfort and hope. Both had rapidly come to the same conclusion, although neither knew exactly where Dart was.

Peek could sense the fishing boat and the chaotic mass of herring writhing within the nets as they drew ever tighter. But where were they? A dolphin's acoustic sense was the best in the sea, but they cannot detect the fine, strong weave of a fishing net. Because it is alien to their world, evolution has not taught them how to recognize it. Such teaching takes eons, and Peek and Bright had only moments. Together they raced through the water, realizing that their own speed could be their doom. Still, Bright's urgency and love for her young and the absolute fear of loss overwhelmed Peek, and he could only swim faster.

Dart heard the whistle again. It was his mother! He needed air and prepared to leap high to signal to his mother that he was fine. He pumped his fluke and shot upward like a rocket in utter joy and anticipation of the reunion. Dolphins are altruistic and give in totally to each other. There is no greater love on earth than that between dolphins, especially a mother and child.

Suddenly, with the glowing surface moments within reach, the young dolphin felt invisible fins closing in around him. His first instinct—his first need—was air, so he continued to press against the imperceptible barrier, but the sea cut into him and he could not reach the surface. Eyes wide with sudden terror, Dart panicked, rolling and spinning, using the evasive maneuvers he'd learned so well to free himself from he knew not what. But these motions only bound him tighter. Bubbles rose around him in an acoustic chaos as his thrashing liberated air from the water. Through it all he heard the desperate whistling of his mother. He needed her, he knew she could save him. He struggled, but the invisible barrier would not yield.

Desperately the young dolphin squealed and whistled. Suddenly he felt the strong nudge of a beak. It was the old one, it was Peek, come to save him. And then there was his mother, nudging him upward—as she had done when he was born, as she had done over and over until he understood how to get air. He hungered for a breath of air as urgent and sweet as his first. Suddenly the others were there, the other females of the home family, all crowding around and tearing at the barrier with their teeth, forcing him upward with their beaks, chirping and whistling their love.

But he could not breathe. Without oxygen, Dart felt dizzy. With the carbon dioxide building up in his young lungs came sharp pain, and he let the air escape. Water rushed in, and he clicked desperately, but his mind clouded. He lost consciousness and drowned.

Peek continued to fight with the nets. But he felt an upward pull, a motion he could not stop. The great nets were being pulled in by the seine boat. Around him were a dozen of his home family members. They all continued tearing at the strands. They could see men at the railings looking and pointing at them. One had a camera, others were yelling. Peek could see that they were pointing at Dart.

Bright gulped air and dove again to try to save her son. Peek knew it was over. It had been far too long for a young dolphin to hold its breath. Peek could no longer sense Dart's thoughts and panicked emotions. The young dolphin's eyes were clouded and lifeless, frozen in the shock of death. For a dolphin, when motion comes to an end, so does life. Peek used his snout to push Bright away from her young. She was too close to the net, which was folding in upon itself as it was pulled on board the boat. The herring, similarly entangled, thrashed violently against the atmosphere the young dolphin had so desperately needed.

Bright let out a continuous resonating wail, and the other females joined in. The sound reverberated through the hull of the fishing boat and caused the humans to pause in wonder and look overboard into the ocean. She watched as her dead son was pulled up and out of the water, away from her world, the twisted form so entangled in the nets—the death wall. How had this happened? Why hadn't she sensed his curiosity a moment sooner? The son she had given birth to, had guided up to the surface for his first breath, had suckled and loved and taught how to fish and play and enjoy the ocean—now his pleading eyes were empty.

They waited. The entire shoal of dolphins circled the fishing boat as the seagulls dove and fed on the spoils. They waited until the men on the boat threw the young dolphin's body back into the sea. Some had seen this before, so they knew to expect it. They surrounded the bruised and twisted body and swam away from the death wall. Peek led the way to a bay along the rocky coast where they would let the body float free and join the waves. The dolphins only ever came to this bay for this purpose, so it was a mournful passage.

On the horizon the storms gathered.

CHAPTER

10

Travel and hear the prayers of the fishes.
Namibian proverb

You are sad today, Peek, I can tell," Jonas said, resting his hand on Peek's back. He had not seen his friend for several days, but he sensed much pain.

Jonas was dressed in his wet suit and wore his mask and snorkel. He had been inspecting some of the supports of the *Atlantic Stroom* as he swam along the surface. The water was very cold, but his wet suit kept out the chill as long as he kept moving. He was very pleased when he felt the gentle nudge of his aquatic friend.

"Catastrophe," Peek intimated to him.

"What is so wrong? What has happened?"

"I have lost one of my young to the wall of death. I was too late. I could not free him. His name was Dart."

Peek's emotions flooded throughout Jonas's mind. It was as if he had lost a son of his own, and tears welled in his eyes. He sensed Peek's thoughts and feelings and understood the magnitude of his loss. A promising young dolphin gone forever, killed for no reason. Jonas was so tuned into Peek that their communications became clearer with each meeting.

Jonas knew immediately what the wall of death had been—purse seine fishing nets. The boats round up fish by motoring in a circle around the school with the seiner in the lead, followed by several skiffs. One of the skiffs pulls the net out of the lead boat and around the school of fish, while the other skiffs motor around the open end, preventing the fish, and the dolphins, from escaping. When the net completes the circle and rejoins the seiner, it is drawn closed from the bottom and hauled aboard. A dolphins might be able to escape at the far end of the net, but once entangled there is little hope. Some countries have outlawed purse seine nets, but many boats still use them. Jonas knew that this was just a small part of the problem. Thousands of dolphins are killed each year—not only drowning in desperation within the nets, but also slaughtered on beaches and poisoned to death by industrial pollution and oil spills.

"Is that why you sought me out?" Jonas asked. "To help stop this murdering of dolphins?"

"That is part of it. We need to know more of the ways of humans. Our trial-and-error way of learning is too costly to our home families. Yes, your knowledge is part of it, but only part, Jonas. Only part."

"And the rest? What else am I to do?"

"Learn also, and wait."

"For what?"

"I myself do not know the full implication of our meetings or what the outcome of our contact will be. To be sure, I have heard of such contact in the past—human and dolphin — but this is my first personal experience with such friendly communication with a human. I have as many questions as you."

"You said you had been captive once. What happened?" Jonas asked. He moved his hand over Peek's soft warm back and could feel where the fish net had recently cut into the dolphin's skin. It was part of the lesson.

"I was young, not yet a full season with my mother. We lived and played in the warm seas that lie into the morning sun, a place farther away than what you call Australia. I have been thinking about it, for my home was a long, long swim."

"You have the markings of a rare dolphin I've heard about in New Zealand. The people who name dolphins would call you a Hector's dolphin," Jonas said.

Peek chirped, a laughing sound. "I prefer my name to this Hector name. Perhaps that is where home was, but that was so long ago now. There was so much to learn in those days. I loved the warmth of the home family and the shared joys of discovering new wonders, for there were more than a dozen of us young ones. We were free and unfettered. Chasing fish and playing in the waves that gathered and crashed on the sandy shores. Leaping to welcome the sun, and again to say farewell with each day."

"It sounds like a paradise," Jonas said, as he imagined the young dolphins in their warm waters and tried to compare it to his local wanderings and explorations as a child.

"Jonas, all the ocean is paradise," Peek said matter-of-factly. "But one day we heard the noise—the sound of propellers driving boats through the water. It was new to us young ones, as it was to my young one Dart. Our mothers warned us and told us not to go near, and we listened. But the noise came toward us. I remember there were two boats, and they were fast and very loud. The home family swam for deep water away from the shore—there were over two hundred dolphins in our home family. The boats raced carelessly into our midst. We were scattered, and the mothers and young—myself included—tired quickly and were cut off from the family.

"One boat chased my mother and me, circling around and driving us underwater. Soon we were exhausted and disoriented. My heart raced. I remember little at that point, but the water was chaotic with the whistling pleas of my mother and other mothers and male dolphins and young. I could not swim any longer, and suddenly there was a net all around me pulling me out of the warm water. My mother pulled at it with her teeth and chirped and screamed in desperation. I could not move. I remember seeing panic in my mother's eyes and hearing panic in her sound."

"It was not a fish net?" Jonas asked.

"No, there were no fish. But it was a net, I know that now. I have seen this many times in the years since. You see, Jonas, the humans wanted *me!* I did not know why. I did not know what humans were then, we had not encountered them before—my mother had, but not I, for I was not yet a season old. Then I was in the air. I remember the hot sun drying my skin, and blood and stinging from my dorsal fin. There were strange noises and strange beings looking at me and touching me. I remember hearing my mother ramming the boat with her beak and whistling desperately—the dull sound resonating through the hull of the boat. The boat raced away, and my mother could not keep up. I was lost, I was alone. Later I realized I had gone into shock, for much time went by and the next thing I knew was in the Pool."

Jonas rested both hands on his friend. His salt tears blended with the salt sea as the cold water washed over Peek's back. "They took you to an aquarium," Jonas said slowly.

"Yes. The Pool. It was a place with no truth. There was no hope in the Pool. The water was tasteless and stale. The barriers were featureless and flat—I could not see them or sound them. I could not swim like I wanted to, for just as I gathered speed I would crash into the barrier."

"Were you alone?" Jonas asked.

"No, not at all. There were others there, but none from my home family. There were dolphins who were lethargic and uncaring. No life in their eyes. Some were aggressive and maniacal and would ram me with their beaks. I quickly learned to stay on the opposite side of the Pool from those bitter creatures. But there was one female, two years older than myself, who took to me, for she recognized me as new. Her name was Glace, and it seemed to me she had once been strong and vibrant, but when we met, her dorsal fin was slack and wrinkled. Glace told me what she knew, that we had to do tricks for food and were not allowed to swim free. She told me which of the humans were okay and which were cruel, although none of them would let us go. I was forced to jump from the water for my food, to swim in circles for food, to do as I was told many times a day—all for dead and tasteless fish. Many humans would be sitting around the Pool watching us do these tricks. Many times a day we had to do this over and over again, always the same. It was exhausting. If I refused, I was locked in a narrow cage and left for a day without food. I almost starved before they broke me.

"For a long time they kept me in a small shallow place where the sun burned my dorsal fin and humans could walk along and touch me. The water was sour and stung my eyes and hurt my stomach. It was humiliating, and I often became sick. My skin became infected and started to blister from the sun and the germs from the humans. Then they put me in an even smaller place where there was no sunlight, and they jabbed me with needles and forced sour liquids into my mouth.

"Finally I healed, and they put me back into the Pool with the other dolphins. There I learned that Glace had died—she committed suicide by ramming her head against the barrier until she died. She did this because she thought I had been taken away and killed. This so affected me that I do not remember anything for a long time after that. I think I almost died as well. Do you know, Jonas, that a sad dolphin will sometimes just stop breathing. We can also stop our hearts if the sadness is too great. But something in me kept me alive. I did not want to forsake the memory of Glace by being defeated by the humans.

"There were other new dolphins brought into the Pool while I was healing. Some were young and frightened, some older and fierce. Most died over the passing seasons, sometimes committing suicide like Glace, other times just succumbing to the germs in the stale water, or they just stopped breathing. There was no hope in the Pool."

Jonas didn't know what to say. He had been to a marine amusement park and had watched the dolphins' show. It was a water circus. It had never occurred to him that in these places the horror of slavery and the breaking of spirits had occurred just to provide tourists with some entertainment. He felt the guilt of humanity upon him and tried to apologize to Peek. But Peek stopped him.

"I know you would not capture us. If you were so inclined, I would not have sought you out. There are many good people. I know this. And I know that one individual does not represent all of us—no matter the home family."

"I am just so sorry this has happened. Where I come from there is a good aquarium that takes in sea creatures needing medical attention, and there is much education that goes on there. But I know many places are not like that," Jonas said. "How did you escape?"

"After my illness I was very weak and could not perform in the Pool. I think the humans recognized this, so they moved me to a new place. This one was separated from the ocean by only a single barrier, a heavy metal net. For the first time since my capture I could taste real ocean water. Sometimes living fish would come in, and I could catch them and once again taste fresh living food. As my body strengthened, my mind also became stronger. I vowed to escape somehow—and I would live only to that end. When the humans left the area in the darkness, I practiced jumping very high, gauging my progress against the height of the barrier. Then one night, on one of my leaps, I discovered I could see over the barrier. I could see moonlight shining across the vast ocean. My heart leapt for joy, and I longed to escape all the more.

But I needed to be stronger to clear the barrier, so I fed on fresh fish and kept practicing.

"One day the humans noticed that I was healthy and tried to lure me into the Pool, away from the ocean. I swam around, evading the poles and nets they threw at me. I had learned of these nets, that I could not sound them, but I could see them. There was much shouting and noise in the air and in the water. I knew it was time, so I swam as fast as possible around and around, gathering speed. Then I leapt into the blue dryness—the air. I saw the ocean beyond and felt the barrier scraping my fluke as I cleared it and dove into the foaming ocean on the other side. The fall stunned me momentarily, but I recovered and forced myself to swim all out toward deeper water. I could hear the noise—that dreaded sound I remembered from my capture— already in the water and giving chase. I swam desperately, staying underwater for long periods of time so the humans could not see me. You see, I now understood some things about them. I had somehow kept from going insane all those seasons in captivity. I had managed to learn and remember and practice for this day of freedom, and I fled with all strength and purpose of any living being."

Jonas said, "And you won your freedom!"

"I did. I could not find my home family after so many seasons away. I fled the warm waters and swam into the sun for many of the sun's cycles—day and night, day and night. I feared I would be captured again. I encountered many boats of all sizes, but none chased me. I saw fishing boats and learned more about the nets by watching them from a distance. I realized that because we could not sound the nets, we could not detect them, which meant they were death traps to us. But at certain distances I could see them.

"So I continued to swim toward the setting sun until I reached these cold waters and found a new home family that would accept me. They took me in, and I shared my knowledge of the Pool and captivity and of humans with them. That was ten seasons ago. This has been my home family ever since. I have saved many from the nets, and when boats came to capture us, we eluded them. Still, some of us die. And now I have lost a young one. My family wonders why I talk to you—a human."

"Why do you, Peek, when all these tragedies have happened to you and your kind?" Jonas asked.

"I have wondered that, but I know that I am driven to you. There is a purpose, in part to gain more knowledge about humans—as we have talked—but there is more, and that I don't fully understand. I know that our species must work together, not enslave us." Peek turned to go.

"I have more questions!" Jonas exclaimed.

"Tomorrow!"

Jonas felt the sudden loss of contact as Peek slipped beneath the ocean's surface and swam off. Peek once again left Jonas with much to ponder. He looked out over the morning ocean at the red and orange display of a rising sun. He thought, *Red sky at morning, sailors take warning.*

CHAPTER

11

Everything that boils will become quiet again.
Namibian proverb

The *Atlantic Stroom* was battened down when the storm hit. The steel supports shuddered under the impact of fifteen-meter waves, and the crew was hunkered down for the blow. It was man's ingenuity against the harsh judge of nature, and the trial was as old as history, with the verdict as varied as a storm's temper.

"What do you think your swimming friend is doing in the storm?" Bebe asked.

Jonas had been cleaning some of his diving equipment and looked up from his work. The two men were in the moon pool area, and the sea welled and frothed a turbulent dark green within the black hole. "I have no idea, Bebe. But you haven't stopped bugging me about it for days."

"Dolphins are good luck! Just curious, that's all."

"Right," Jonas said, expressing his disbelief with a smirk. "Tell me what's on your mind."

"Dolphins are on my mind . . . and yours, I'll wager." Bebe paused as he looked into the seething black hole. The drill platform shuddered as a large wave rolled past the structural supports. "Dolphins often save men from the sea. But what we saw with that sinking Portuguese fishing boat, well, that has never been heard of before."

"I know, I've been going over that in my mind, too," Jonas said as he looked toward Bebe. "It gives us sailors hope if we were to fall overboard. And besides, now we all have our own firsthand account of friendly dolphins."

"Ah, my friend, you can already swim as good as a dolphin. You spend half your time in the water as it is," Bebe said.

"Yes, too much, perhaps. But the dolphin keeps me company—everyone loves a dolphin."

Bebe raised an eyebrow and said, "Do you know of the boy and the dolphin in Africa?"

"No," Jonas said. He smiled, sensing another one of Bebe's Namibian lessons coming on.

"This is not a happy story, but it is one that foretells the future . . . or a future," Bebe said.

Jonas sighed. "I was hoping it was a happy one. I've heard so many sad ones lately."

"Well, it is *only* a story, not necessarily a true one. But there might be a lesson in it!"

"There is a lesson in everything you say, Bebe." Jonas patted his friend on the shoulder. "So, please, tell me your story."

Bebe nodded, and smiled at the compliment. "You see, there was a village on the western coast of Africa where the men and boys would swim into the sea to fish. The boys of the village had a contest every day, and the winner was the boy who could swim farthest from the shore.

"One day the boy in the lead met a dolphin as he swam farther and farther out. The boy had no fear, for some say they could talk to one another, but of course that couldn't be so!" Bebe raised an eyebrow and looked at Jonas.

"What?" Jonas said, balking at his friend's unspoken question.

Bebe laughed a deep laugh. He continued, "The dolphin carried the boy even farther out, then swam back to the shore where the boy could climb off and walk easily to the beach.

"Every day thereafter the boy would meet the dolphin and swim in the sea. After a time the word got out, and many people from all around began coming to the village to see the dolphin and the boy. It was an amazing sight, and the word spread farther. Soon so many people were coming to the village that the elders became distressed. The village had become crowded with strangers. The local families were nervous from all the confusion. The village elders met to talk over the problem. Rather than send the people away, which did not seem to work because they kept coming back, they decided to send the dolphin away. But how?

"The solution they arrived at was to kill the dolphin so all the visitors would leave. This they did, and the boy was forever sad after that. He accosted the elders, saying, 'How can you kill something so kind and wonderful just because the kindness does not suit you?' And now we find the fishermen killing the dolphins to get their fish. Even now we have not learned our lesson."

This last comment put Jonas in a low mood, for he had learned from Peek that this was so and what the nets did to dolphins, especially to Peek's son. "Yeah, Bebe, we have not all learned. But some of us are learning. I can only be as hopeful as a dolphin I know."

"Be cautious, my friend. Mankind is rarely kind or fair. Do not let your dolphin friend find harm's way."

Jonas looked up at Bebe and was flooded with a feeling of understanding from his companion. What did Bebe know? thought Jonas, and then he said, "I would never let harm come to this dolphin."

The dolphins swam north into sheltered bays to weather nature's attack. For the duration of the storm, they would stay close to one another to keep the young ones safe, riding the steep swells in the sheltered water with practiced patience.

Peek had always liked a good storm. He was seldom in danger, unless caught out in the open ocean. Sometimes the wind blew so much water off the wave crests that it was difficult to breathe. But like all dolphins, Peek could sense the change in air pressure indicating an advancing storm, and he always led the family to a sheltered bay. Sometimes he shared the calmer waters with minke whales or fur seals. It was a time when species that normally did not interact much would learn of one another: the young ones would play together for a while, and the older ones would exchange knowledge and news. The different species learned each other's languages, and practical cooperation had evolved, especially in this new era of humans claiming the oceans.

Peek was speaking with an ancient fur seal named Whiskers. Whiskers had many scars from defending his harem. He had a gray muzzle, which marked him as a wise and experienced veteran of many, many seasons. The old seal, being widely known, was revered by all mammals of the ocean and had held many conversations with Peek over the years. The seal was very interested in Peek's experiences with humans, since he had seen many of his seal herd also captured or slaughtered by them.

"And you can understand this human?" Whiskers was saying.

"Amazingly, yes," Peek said. "You recall my account of years of captivity? Well, this human is not like those who trapped me. He is more akin to us sea mammals, attuned to the ocean, and more open-minded. I saved him from Old Death."

Whiskers shuddered visibly at the mention of the name. Old Death had taken many young seals from his herd over the years. The great white would shoot up from below like a rocket and ambush an unsuspecting seal, then toss it violently into the air. Seals rarely escaped such attacks. He himself had narrowly cheated

Old Death by a whisker's length when the shark had surprised the herd. "How did you save him?" asked the old seal.

"Diversion, the usual method. That old shark is very mad and still very stubborn. He's down around the Cape Town now, or so I have heard, threatening human swimmers and some of your distant kin."

"Well, what do you expect from a fish, especially one who's been around as long as time itself?" Whiskers rolled over in the swell, keeping his nose in the air to breathe freely. He could hear Peek's chatter language by keeping an ear underwater. Peek swam lazily around him and continued to talk in his dolphin way.

"That fish will be back. The dolphins to the south say his habit is to leave the cape and continue around the coast to feed and breed until he is satisfied—if that is even possible. I would not want to be a human on those sandy beaches these days."

"Better them than us," Whiskers said as he rolled again in the water. The ocean swell was big, but not breaking in the sheltered bay. The wind ruffled his short, dark brown fur. "Now back to this human. What will become of your communication with it?"

"I don't know. I have heard legends of such encounters, but as I told the human—who goes by the name of Jonas—I understand about as much as he does. Time will tell."

"It always does, Peek, it always does. So, can the human stop the whale boats and the fishing boats and the slaughtering of my brethren for fur and hides?"

"I think probably not. He is not involved with such humans, and I don't know how the various humans communicate or influence each other. There are so many of them, you know."

"Hmmm. I see your point. It's probably like us trying to reason with an orca when they want to catch our young. Almost nothing is more powerful than an appetite."

"And the humans have a big one," Peek said.

"I wonder how the animals on land fare with all these humans around. It must be a place of constant terror. We risk our lives just to sun on the rocks and bring our young ashore to escape Old Death's jaws. I can't imagine being on land all the time."

"I can't imagine it at all," Peek chattered and made a sound as near a laugh as a dolphin could do. "But this human has my attention, and I will let you know how things go."

"Please, my friend, be careful, for my heart would be hollow without you in this ocean." Whiskers slapped the water once with a flipper to signal it was time to end the chat and go and check up on his harem. One must never leave the young ones alone too long, especially the young bulls—they would get ideas with all the young cows about!

The storm abated two days later. By then the crew of the *Atlantic Stroom* was ready for some stable footing. They began tending to the minor bits of weather damage on the drilling platform. Jonas's earlier repairs to the pontoon supports had held firm. The crew knew that in the months to come construction would begin for the floating docks and oil delivery port. The rig was always busy.

Peek and his home family were glad to wander free of the sheltered bay, for although they enjoyed the seals, they were guests there, and Peek knew the old saying—that a guest is like the waters of a bay . . . he should not be stagnant. Besides, the herring would be running after the storm, and that was an opportunity not to be missed.

CHAPTER

12

When you have luck, hold it firmly in your hand and take it home.

Namibian proverb

The evening was aflame with red and orange and gold as the sun struck the horizon in a silent brilliance. *Red sky at night, sailor's delight.* The ocean was a mirror to the spectacle of nature. Maintenance on the drill platform meant the pumps and drills were shut down, so only the occasional muffled clang of steel and the distant hum of the power plant invaded the otherwise dead quiet.

Down near the water Jonas sat alone and searched the western horizon. He wondered if the dolphins would jump out of the water to catch the last bit of warmth before the ocean doused the sun's light. And suddenly there they were! He could just make out more than a dozen shapes leaping in joy from the water. They were so distant he could not hear the splashes. Jonas felt a warmth rush through him, and he inexplicably got goose bumps.

Jonas sat by the water as the colors darkened and the first stars winked in the inky blackness. There would be a full moon tonight, but for now the stars were the planet's night lights. The sea was so clear that the Milky Way was perfectly mirrored, and looking down at the water he identified constellations in reverse. They were like diamonds spread across the earth. He recalled Bebe's descriptions of the diamonds recovered from the coast, among the desert dunes, and by divers in the sea. So much wealth in man's eyes, but none of it of any value to the dolphins. Jonas chuckled to himself at something Peek had told him earlier: *We don't build*

88

things like you, but we also don't pollute the oceans like you do. Which is better? Which is smarter?

The mirror of the ocean was broken by the swish of a fin. It was Peek. Jonas had sensed his presence even before he saw him this time and felt warmed, made happy by the visit. Peek realized the heightened awareness in Jonas as well. The dolphin nuzzled Jonas's hand and rocked his head back.

"What's this, my friend?" Jonas asked as he reached for something in Peek's beak. It was a large stone. Jonas held it up in the light cast down from the drill platform. It was a huge diamond, and it filled the whole of Jonas's hand! He sat up and eyed it with amazement. "Where did you get this?"

"They are all over certain parts of the seafloor. They are especially common where the Orange River drains into the sea. I brought it as a gift. I have watched many divers spend much time underwater collecting these with their hoses and pumps—they suck up the sand and these shiny stones. When I find big ones in my explorations I put them in a place the divers never go. I reasoned that if they can no longer find these shiny stones, then they will go away. But this one is for you, a gift, because I now understand humans need such stones for their civilization. Besides, I do not want you to go away." Peek nodded happily at having brought such a thing to Jonas.

"I don't know what to do with it!"

"What do other humans do with the stones they collect?"

"Sell them, I guess. But I don't know who to sell it to."

Peek chirped and squeaked, a laughing sound, and said, "Then just keep it as a gift. At the very least its sparkle in the sunlight is pleasing to the eye. It is the brightest of the stones we find in the sea."

Jonas hefted the huge diamond in his hand. It must be worth a fortune, he thought. With the money from such a thing I could do some good. Possibly some good for these dolphins!

Peek chirped again, passing along his feeling that he was proud of Jonas for thinking such thoughts. It was further proof to the dolphin that Jonas had a good heart.

Jonas told Peek to wait a moment, and he climbed up the access ladder to the mezzanine deck. He slipped the diamond into his locker, then grabbed his wet suit, mask, snorkel, flippers, a high-intensity waterproof flashlight, and an inflatable life vest with a GPS microchip. He climbed back down to water level and, quickly and quietly as possible, slipped back to the water's edge without running into any of the other crew.

"What are you up to?" Peek asked.

"Putting on my blubber. You and I are going for a swim!"

"Marvelous. But don't you need your air hoses and all the other things you hook up to when you dive?"

"Nope. You breathe air, and so do I, so let's make sure we come up every few minutes or so.

"Do you want more of the shiny stones?" Peek asked, curious as to Jonas's sudden interest in swimming.

"Nope. I do not. I just want to go swimming with you. We can talk and look around. We're in water too deep for me to dive to the bottom anyway. I just want to be in your world for a few hours, that's all. I've wanted to do this for some time. Everyone's working on various things on the drill platform, and I am not needed tonight. So, shall we swim? The moon, a full one, will be up soon."

Peek leapt from the water and sent a great cold wave of the sea splashing down upon Jonas. The answer was a definite *YES!*

The South Atlantic is cold, but Jonas's thick wet suit kept out the chill for a long while. He was in excellent shape and swam with an ease surpassed only by Peek's own aquatic grace. They swam away from the semi into the lazy surface current. Now and then Jonas would hook his hand around Peek's dorsal fin and be towed along. They would surface and breathe together a couple times a minute, and Jonas found the rhythm perfectly suitable to his needs. Sometimes they would dive, holding their breath for several minutes or even longer. Jonas felt the water as never before. It became part of him, flowed with him and seemingly through him. He sensed small perturbations in the currents and countered them to help his forward progress. He rolled and twisted when Peek did. He could not, however, leap from the water as Peek could, though he desperately wished he were able to perform such acrobatics.

As he held onto Peek, he had a sense of fulfillment. He felt at home—as though he had finally found home. Working in the water as a diver had never been quite enough, Jonas now realized. He wanted the camaraderie, to become part of the community in this new kingdom. Jonas sensed he was on the fringes of such a gift. He held on. The sea glowed green around them in the night with phosphorescent plankton.

Peek also felt a surge of fulfillment. His mind merged and flowed among the thoughts of the human, and he gained new understanding of both their worlds—one of water and the other of land. He now understood his need to seek out the human, and why much of his life had been unsettled—for it could not be complete without this link. And here it now occurred—the telepathic connection between two species. It was a rare, some say impossible, thing. Yet here it was, the real deal. Peek sensed that it was a significant leap for the beings of Earth. He believed that it had not happened like this for a long time. Maybe this was what the ancient gods that Jonas told him about had experienced.

Their mingled thoughts and fluid motions of swimming in unison through the dark Atlantic were suddenly interrupted by a bone-rattling growl. The acoustic assault pierced the water all around them.

Jonas stopped swimming immediately and poked his head out of the water. "Peek! What was that?"

"Whales. Big ones. The deep seekers, the ones you call sperm whales. There is an entire pod here with young."

"That is some sound they give out. It really hurts!"

"That is because there are orcas here also. This is a dangerous place, for the orcas are hunting the young sperm whales."

Jonas reached out to his friend's dorsal fin. "Are we in danger?"

"Orcas always mean danger. Let me investigate. I will gauge the threat and return in a moment," Peek said, and like a torpedo he shot off into the dark ocean.

Jonas was suddenly cut off from Peek's reassuring knowledge and experience. The full moon had risen in the clear night sky and turned the ocean from a black void to a glistening silver surface. He realized he was floating alone in the vast Atlantic. The lights of the drill platform were distant specks on the southern horizon—*my God, I must be fifteen kilometers from the rig!* Panic surged up in Jonas, for this feeling was new to him—being alone in a black sea. He steadied his breath and concentrated on slowing his heart rate. *If the dolphins can control their heart, then so can I!* He felt himself relax, and again he became part of the vast ocean. But this was suddenly disrupted as well.

Just a few hundred meters distant, the placid sea erupted as a huge black form rose up and came crashing back to the water. It was an orca! Its white markings seemed to glow in the moonlight. Then another, and another. There was an entire pod of them, and they were so close to Jonas. He felt panic welling up again as he sensed the pressure in the water from the massive cetaceans swimming nearby.

Suddenly Peek was at his side. "Jonas! We must seek refuge. Grab on to my dorsal fin!"

"Where? Where out here is there refuge?" Jonas thought as he fumbled through the water to link up with Peek.

"The whales!"

"You don't mean the orcas!"

"No, they are hunting now, they are the danger. We must find refuge with the sperm whales. There is safety in numbers." Peek pumped his fluke, and the two of them sped through the water diagonally away from the orcas.

The water rushed around Jonas and filled his mask. He choked on seawater as he cleared his snorkel and gulped air every chance he could. Suddenly there was an enormous living island beside him, and he nearly lost his grip on Peek as panic and surprise ran rampant through his nervous system.

"That is the Old One, Jonas. He is the alpha of this pod. He has no fear. He is older than age. He dives deep to battle the giant squid. And he offers us refuge among his pod."

"How many are here?" Jonas said in awe, as he saw dark shapes breaching around him. The sperm whales' wet skin glistened silver in the brilliant starlight. The air was filled with the sounds of the whales breathing as geysers of moisture erupted from their blowholes.

"This pod has about thirty whales. Four are juveniles, and the pod is taking a defensive position as the orcas approach." The massive whales glowed ghostly gray in the reflected light of the moon.

Jonas cleared his mask and looked around at the whales as they seemed to organize themselves in a pattern. The water pressure changed and the currents shifted as they moved their massive bodies around and under the juveniles. Peek and Jonas mingled with the young, who were themselves big enough to overturn a medium-sized boat. Jonas realized that the sperm whales were forming a defensive circle around them, their massive heads and toothy jaws pointed out toward the oncoming orcas. The aggressors also had rather toothy jaws. Several of the sperm whales swam below the pod to deflect any attack from below. He realized this was a well-organized, intelligent, and obedient group of animals. *Safety in numbers!* Their basso chatter and high-pitched clicks resonated through the water, and the juveniles kept absolutely silent. They were the real target of the orcas. Any type of injury would be the kiss of death in the deep ocean, as the orcas would simply pursue a wounded juvenile until it weakened or died of its wounds. Jonas also realized he could be one of the victims. He felt mortal and fragile among these behemoths.

"Be calm, Jonas," Peek chirped. "The Old One will protect us. I have warned him many times of approaching orcas. We are old friends, and he is experienced."

"How many orcas are there?" Jonas asked, not really wanting to know. It was like opening a dark closet to see how many spooks were there—you were too afraid to do it, but you *had* to know.

"This is a big pod of orcas, perhaps fifteen or twenty. They approach in columns, so we can't sound them easily. Also they splash about to confuse the echoes from our soundings. They are experienced, but they will not attack when the whales are in this position because the teeth of the sperm whale can kill an orca, and the orcas' intent here is not to kill the entire pod, just to get the young."

A juvenile near Peek groaned softly with a series of deep clucking and clicking sounds at overhearing Peek's description of the impending attack. Peek nuzzled the huge child reassuringly and apologized for frightening it. There was a sharp grunt from one of the mothers warning the young whale to remain quiet. The orcas must not learn exactly where the juveniles were within the pod.

Suddenly the water was filled with ear-deafening boomings and acoustic growls. The male sperm whales bellowed at the approaching orcas. The sound was so intense it would certainly inflict discomfort and some pain on the enemy. As the ruckus continued, the whales on guard beneath the pod stayed under-water for fifteen minutes and then traded positions with males at the surface. The orcas approached cautiously, and their columns split around the pod of sperm whales. Jonas could tell where the orcas were by the sudden eruption of bellowing from the sperm whales.

As the orcas split up, he sensed their numbers and realized he was doing so through Peek. *How many? What! More than twenty! More than thirty! More than forty!*

The sperm whales thrashed about as they realized the huge number of orcas in the attacking pod. The Old One remained confident and relayed this confidence to his pod through a long stream of clicks and shrieks. And now Jonas saw the old alpha rise up, his massive scarred dome a monument to survival. Jonas could make out disc-shaped scars, tattoos from his battles with giant squid deep in the oceans. But the orcas continued to circle. Several dove beneath the pod, only to resurface, diverted by those on guard below.

Suddenly to one side a number of orcas charged forward. The sperm whales bellowed and crowded together. The Old One clicked loudly—it was a ruse, an attempt to open up another side of their defense. The sperm whales remained in formation—a tight circle, heads out and down to fend off the enemy. More orcas charged again, and again they feinted and turned away even as others charged from yet another direction.

Jonas was full of both fascination and terror. He could sense the complex movement and the cacophony of whale sounds—both defenders and attackers—through his telepathic link with Peek. But his own human senses could also feel the surges of water and the life force around him as these huge beings responded to each other. The ocean's surface was a riotous chop of waves and foam from the great sloshing about of the whales. It was all Jonas could do to maintain his position among the juveniles and keep his snorkel above water to breathe.

An orca broke through the lower defenses and tried to swim up under the juveniles. Several of the females quickly herded their young to one side of the inner circle, and suddenly the mass of young whales nearly crushed Peek and Jonas against the flukes of the outer circle defenders. Somehow, though, the whales were aware of them, and at the last instant small patches of water opened up in which Peek and Jonas could swim and breathe. The attacking orca, sensing the shift within the circle, veered off to swim clear of the other guards.

Then the lead orca was rammed by one of the defenders, and the water was filled with its sharp grunts of pain. Jonas could hear loud cracking sounds—the orca's ribs breaking. The impact sent the killer whale off to the side where it spewed a blood-tinged, silvery spray from its blowhole. Even as this happened, still others charged the fringes. The orcas kept their order and, as if guided by the most formidable of human military strategists, probed the defenses of the sperm whales.

Hours passed, and Jonas finally climbed onto the back of one of the older whales to rest his arms and legs. It was not a smooth ride, but it offered some refuge. This new vantage point was even more terrifying, however, for the night had worn away and the first gray light of dawn revealed just how many orcas were circling with their stiff, upright dorsal fins and distinctive white and black markings. They crashed about in the water, and Jonas realized that such action created a chaotic wall of bubbles through which other charging orcas could not be detected until the last instant. This gave the sperm whales only moments to react and fill the gaps in their defenses.

There would be several points of attack around the defensive circle at once. Then the fins of half a dozen orcas would vanish beneath the sea and suddenly reappear right in front of the sperm whales. There was a brief moment in which the attacker would gauge the defender—*Can I get by you? Can I defeat you?* So far the sperm whales had held their ground. With all the acoustic chaos, every sea creature for kilometers around knew what was going on. Jonas could see several sharks in the distance, probing the scene. But even these ancient hunters had enough sense to swim clear of such an aggressive pod of orcas.

Three swift, young orcas suddenly broke through the lower guards. Two shot up into the inner circle. One was immediately deterred by a severe ramming from a defender, and a second one turned outward in retreat at the last moment. The third orca broke through and was suddenly in among the juveniles and Peek and Jonas. Jonas found himself face to face with an enormous killer whale. This was the last thing the killer whale had expected ... *a human!* The orca paused in its confusion as it sounded Jonas. It knew of humans, even respected their power. The orca thought: *But this is only one. What should I do? What is a human doing here?*

Peek sensed the orca's hesitation and lunged at the attacker with a sudden burst of speed. The beak of a dolphin delivers a sharp blow when aimed at the tender underbelly of a whale. This sudden pain further confused the orca, and by then two of the female sperm whales were upon it. The first closed her toothy jaws down upon the fluke of the invader. This is a deadly wound to any whale, for it weakens its chances of escape. Now there was blood in the water. The second female accelerated at a frightening speed and rammed the stunned orca with such force that the attacker was literally tossed out of the inner circle. The smack from the collision was deafening. The outer circle of males continued to batter the orca as they reestablished the perimeter.

The sharks in the area flitted about with excitement at the smell of blood in the water, and several made senseless forays toward the wounded orca. One even managed to tear into the wounded fluke before the massive jaws of an enraged elder orca crushed the shark and flung it far from the injured pod member. That shark became a feast for the others.

A second failed attack and injury to yet another orca was the turning point in the siege. As if bowing to the Old One, the orcas suddenly turned tail in unison and swam slowly away from the sperm whales. The Old One, suspecting foul play, kept the pod in its defensive formation until their soundings assured him that the orcas had indeed retreated.

"You!" bellowed the Old One toward Jonas.

Jonas was buzzing with adrenaline and fear and relief. He clung to Peek, wondering what was happening now.

"We of the deep have never had anything good happen when we encountered humans. But you within our midst have saved our young from certain death. The orca was confused by your presence—as were we before Peek explained to us who you were—and those brief moments allowed us to expel the attacker." The enormous whale slowly swam around until its huge eye stared at Jonas. Jonas gazed at it in awe of this enormous marine mammal. He had a fleeting thought about the meaning of his own name—Jonas. The great whale continued to communicate with him, much the way Peek did, and said, "You will not be for gotten to any of us, and you are always welcome to take refuge among us." The Old One chirped additional appreciation to Peek.

The juveniles chattered to their mothers. It was all very exciting, now that the orcas had fled. And even more so to have a human in their midst. There would be stories about this day, the young whales clicked and chirped among themselves. The pod turned in unison and headed in the opposite direction of the retreating orcas. It is never wise to linger when there are orcas about.

Soon Peek and Jonas were swimming southward alone. Nothing needed to be said. Jonas had been accepted by the whales! Peek was proud. Jonas was stunned and emotionally overwhelmed by the events of the night. It was some hours before they were back at the semi and Jonas hauled his sore and exhausted body out of the sea. He immediately collapsed into a deep sleep of exhaustion on the lower mooring deck.

CHAPTER

13

Don't teach the swallow to fly.
Namibian proverb

Jonas awoke to the bright lights of the semi's infirmary. He tried to sit up, but dull pains coursed through every muscle in his body. He felt a hand on his shoulder gently holding him down.

"You are with us again, I see," Bebe said in his deep voice, his massive frame outlined by the bright ceiling lights.

"Yeah, what's going on?" Jonas asked in a voice cracked and raspy. His throat stung from salt water, his eyes were puffy, and his lips were cracked and stinging.

"We wanted to ask you the same thing. You were missing for eight hours," another voice said. It was the doctor.

"Eight . . ."

"That's right, friend," Bebe said. "I found you on the mooring deck this afternoon. You were in your wet suit, passed out, dehydrated, and suffering from exposure. You're lucky there were no high seas. You would have been swept overboard. It's still dead calm outside."

"Eight hours?" Jonas realized it must have been much longer than that since he had slipped into the water the night before. He must have been at sea with Peek for more than sixteen hours!

"Dead right," Bebe said.

"You didn't just fall overboard, Jonas," the doctor said. He was a tall, slender man with neatly combed brown hair, perfectly parted on the right side, and a young, well-scrubbed face. "The captain would like to know what happened. You could well have died if Bebe hadn't found you."

"Uh, I was . . ." Jonas started to say, and winced at the pain of sore muscles. He pushed himself up so he could lean on an elbow and talk to the two men. His eyes grew accustomed to the bright lights. "I was just out swimming for a while."

Bebe and the doctor exchanged glances, both with raised eyebrows. Bebe said, "Just out for a swim?"

"Well, yeah, and the, uh, the current caught me, I was dragged . . ."

"You know better than that," the doctor said. "You're the most experienced diver I've ever met, and no one in their right mind would go for a *swim* in this ocean at *night! Alone!* "

Jonas shrugged sheepishly and slumped back in the bed. It sounded pretty crazy to him as well, but what really happened would be unbelievable to these men. He waited until the doctor went into the next room to check up on another patient and he was alone with Bebe.

"And during that swim did you see any dolphins?" Bebe asked, with a comical lilt in his deep Namibian voice. "You are almost at home, but you are not a fish, Jonas. On land we do not teach swallows to fly. You should not try to teach dolphins to swim!"

"Point taken," Jonas said, and laughed briefly until the dull pain of sore belly muscles caused him to groan. "It was amazing, Bebe. I swam with that dolphin for a long time."

"You know," Bebe said quietly, "your GPS locator was on the whole time." He paused a moment to let that fact sink into Jonas's brain. "I plotted your route on the map. Jonas, you went as far out as thirty-five kilometers from the *Atlantic Stroom*. How is that possible?" Bebe asked quietly.

"Sit close, my friend, I have a story to tell you," Jonas said. Bebe pulled up a chair and straddled it next to the bed to listen as Jonas told him of his encounter with the whales.

It was a couple of days before Jonas was up and about. Swimming for nearly a full day in the cold waters of the Atlantic would have killed almost anyone, and he still couldn't believe what he had experienced and lived through. It seemed that the strength he had drawn from Peek was enough to sustain him while in the water, but once he was back on the semi's deck his body had succumbed to total exhaustion.

The placid seas had once again turned rough, and yet another storm was brewing to the south of Cape Town. Jonas's schedule began to return to normal, although the dive captain restricted him from underwater work for a solid week following his strange episode of exhaustion. On the day he was assessed as fit for diving, he was down in the black hole area checking his gear when a call came to him over the intercom. He was being summoned to the helideck.

"What have you done now?" Willy said, followed by a chuckle. Willy was crouched down by one of the winch motors, finishing repairs. He looked at Jonas, who had become even more of a celebrity on board, what with the shark attack, the fishermen rescued by dolphins, and then his mysterious nighttime swim in the ocean.

"I don't know," Jonas said, as he put his gear back into his locker.

"You're not gonna pull another *Jonas*, are ya?" Willy said, and then let go a hearty laugh. The crew had started to call any dumb stunt "a Jonas," but it was delivered with the brotherly affection of camaraderie that exists between men in tough jobs and intense situations.

"All right already, I won't go for a swim at night. At least not for a week!" He reached for his hard hat and tucked it under his arm.

Willy gave Jonas a comical thumbs up and turned back to his work.

Jonas made his way up the steep steps and through the various decks to the main work area. He stopped at the hatch to put on his hard hat and then walked out onto the main deck. A cloud-laden sky met him, and he paused and turned his face into the stiff breeze. It held the scent of the sea, punctuated with a tinge of oil and lubricant from the topside mechanicals. It also held the restlessness of an oncoming storm.

The helideck sat aft on the *Atlantic Stroom,* and Jonas could see the bulky form of the project's workhorse helicopter, a yellow and red CH-149 Cormorant. The old Canadian Air Force chopper had been recycled for use on oil rigs and could fly in any weather. It was outfitted with all sorts of emergency response and sea rescue equipment. Its five long rotors sagged in resting position but flexed uncomfortably in the windy atmosphere. Jonas could see the pilot standing by the sliding side door on the starboard side of the chopper, presumably waiting for him. He could see that there were people inside. He thought perhaps he was being summoned to Cape Town for some reason. Jonas bounded up the metal steps to the platform.

"Captain?" Jonas said.

"Yeah, Brandon." The pilot extended a hand in greeting. "You Jonas?" he asked, with a friendly, singsong northern Canadian accent.

"Yes sir," Jonas said, and shook the pilot's hand. "You've got some weather coming in."

"Yes, soon enough. This old bug-eyed bird can handle it though."

"I hear you have a message for me."

"Indeed. I was in the Cape Town office this morning, eh, and these two women walked in. I'm thinking to myself, wow, Brandon, your ship has come in, eh. And they're all anxious, and saying they have to see this Jonas Jeremy James fella, eh. Now I heard about ya, 'cause of you and that rescue with them dolphins and stuff. Well, these two women had gotten some kind of permission from Van Stuer, so . . ." The pilot pushed the door open all the way, and there sat two women with big smiles on their faces, peering out at Jonas.

"Madeleine?" Jonas gasped.

Jonas's sister unbuckled her seatbelt and leaped out of the chopper into his arms. "I missed you, Jonas! Mary B and I just had to come and see you!"

Mary Beth climbed out of the chopper with the help of the pilot's hand and gave Jonas a big smile.

"But how did you even get permission?"

"To fly in? I saw Mr. Van Stuer's name in that *New York Times* article about you, and so I took a chance. I called him. Johan, that's what he said I should call him, you know he's the general manager, well, he is a big fan of yours. He was so excited that Jonas's sister could visit." Madeleine smiled a smile Jonas knew well, one that he could never say no to. Madeleine always got her way.

Jonas laughed and then looked to Madeleine's companion. "So, who's your friend."

"Well, she's your fiancée. Anyway . . ." Madeleine held up her index finger over Jonas's lips as he started to protest. "Now let me finish. That's what we told Mr. Van Stuer, otherwise he wouldn't let us both on—family only, he said. So, Jonas meet Mary Beth, my very best friend from Mystic. We teach at the same school."

Mary Beth gave Jonas a quick hug and spoke breathlessly in rapid, run-on sentences. "I'm so glad to meet you. I've heard all about what you do and this is an amazing place and you actually see dolphins in the ocean, *wow*, and we saw Cape Town, *whoa*, and that helicopter ride, *whew*, that was a first, I've never been much out of Mystic before, but this is really something. It's so nice to meet you *finally*."

Jonas smiled at her. "Uh, we're not really getting married are we?"

"Oh, my! No! I mean, like NO! Well . . ." Mary Beth smiled warmly at Jonas, as though she considered the thought might not be a bad one. She leaned into him, her hand on his arm and whispered in his ear, "Unless . . ." she trailed off as if the thought had caught a telltale wind.

Jonas chuckled and raised his eyebrows. "Okay, well, that'll free up the afternoon then," he said. He paused and looked around, then said, "So, let me get you two settled for your visit, and then I can show you around." He picked up their bags and led his unexpected visitors to the guest cabins.

A cold wind caught Madeleine's long hair and whipped it up like a warning flag. She paused at the top of the companionway and looked out over the metallic gray ocean. White caps were forming on the waves, and the sky was overcast with a pall of gunmetal stratus clouds. She knew enough about weather from her seaside life in Mystic to know what was coming.

CHAPTER

14

*What is useful for the next life is not
useful for this life.*
Namibian proverb

The four of them sat around the small table in Jonas's cabin. It was long after dinner, and Bebe had joined Jonas and Madeleine and Mary Beth for a cup of tea and a long chat in the late night peace and quiet. They had been talking about dolphins for hours. Outside the wind had picked up to an alarming degree, and rain pelted the porthole glass.

"It will be a Force 10 by morning, no doubt," Bebe said.

"A Force 10? That's pretty bad, isn't it, Jonas?" Madeleine asked, as she watched the rain splattering on the window.

"A very rough sea, that's what it means," Jonas said. "Oh, I wish you hadn't come out now, I'd feel safer if you were ashore. This is the stormy season here."

"But it's springtime," Madeleine said.

"In the northern hemisphere, yes, but down here south of the equator, it's autumn, and that means storms. Big ones. We've had one a week for the past month."

"Wouldn't miss this for the world!" Mary Beth proclaimed. She was definitely enjoying the excitement. She also liked sitting close to Jonas.

Jonas had decided he quite liked Mary Beth. She was very smart, full of odd facts about all manner of things—one of the benefits of being a good teacher—and she had a caring comfort about her. It was easy to see why she and Madeleine had hit it off.

They could be sisters. "Well, then," Jonas said, "I have something to show you all, but you must not tell a soul. Promise?" There were nods all around.

"You must realize," Bebe said to Madeleine in his deep voice, "that Jonas has been full of surprises lately. No telling what he's got up his sleeve this time."

"You be the judge, Bebe, for this is something I'd like to give to Maddy, but you'll know more about it than I." Jonas stood up from the table and walked over to his desk. He pulled open a drawer and retrieved a small canvas bag. He held it up as he returned to the table and sat down. "This is the surprise," he said. Jonas reached into a canvas bag and pulled out the gift Peek had given him. Everyone's eyes grew wide with amazement. Bebe let out a slow breath and carefully reached for the diamond.

"By the sands of the Namib! Jonas, where did you find such a stone?" Bebe held it up and could see the flawless nature of the brilliant white diamond. It was a huge octahedron crystal, with natural frosted coating on some of the facets. But Bebe looked into the magnificent brilliant space of the diamond's interior. There was not a single inclusion or fracture to be found in the gem. It had a perfect octahedral shape and seemed to glow even in the cabin's light. "By the sands!"

"That's enormous!" Madeleine said.

"Dead right. Hundreds of carats," Bebe whispered.

Madeleine exchanged amazed looks with Mary Beth and then settled her gaze back upon the stone. "Jonas, where did you get this?"

"The dolphin brought it up from the deep. It is a gift, and I give it to you, Maddy."

Bebe raised an eyebrow. "You're sure you didn't pick it up with the submersible on one of your dives?"

Jonas chuckled and winked at Bebe. "Yes, I'm sure, my friend. The dolphin really did retrieve it. So what do you think?"

"I think you have a smart dolphin. Can he get one of these for me?" Bebe laughed loudly. "By the sands of the Namib, this stone is worth a fortune."

"Is it worth more than a million dollars?" Mary Beth asked.

"Dead right," Bebe said. "Far more than that."

"Well, Maddy, it's yours. I don't need it, and I want you to have it. I do have one request, however."

Madeleine was stunned. She looked back to Jonas after gawking at the diamond. "Sure, Jonas, whatever you want. But this is from your dolphin friend; won't he be disappointed?"

"Not in the least. He just figured out that humans like these things and brought me one. But the condition I place upon this gift to you is that some of the money be used to help dolphins. I'm not sure how it should be used—we'll figure that out later—but it must be used wisely. Maybe when you're home you can donate a lot of the money to the Mystic Aquarium to help dolphins. You could even tie that into an educational thing at your school."

"I promise, Jonas. I don't know what else to say, this is incredible."

"Ah, but it is not so easy," Bebe said. "First of all, you must tell no one of this stone, or you will become the target of thieves. Worse yet, it is illegal to own such a stone in Namibia or South Africa. It will be difficult to smuggle it out to your home in America. But once you get it there, you must take it immediately to a trustworthy diamond cutter."

"I feel like a criminal!" Madeleine said.

"But you are not, for this stone is unknown to any man and has not been stolen from any man. Therefore, it is yours, free and clear, but you must be cautious," Bebe said.

"Well, perhaps you can help us, Bebe, for I think the money can be put to good use. Are you willing?" Jonas knew he could trust Bebe, who was already wealthy from diamonds. He also knew his friend would know the appropriate contacts to make.

"I would be honored. But by entering the world of diamonds you will learn that all thieves are in the diamond business, though not everyone in it is a thief! You must learn to be a good judge of character."

The *Atlantic Stroom* shook from a sudden gust of wind.

Bebe looked up from the diamond and toward the porthole into the darkening night. "We should all get ready for the storm," he said in his deep voice.

Peek's home family retreated again to the sanctuary of the bays so that the full force of the storm would not find them. The seals crowded into their rocky shelters as well and barked at the winds in fear and frustration. The whales were long gone, staying far below the surface waves for long periods of time. Just as the humans on their metal island had battened down for the blow, so too had the sea mammals prepared for the night.

But something kept Peek from remaining in the shelter of the bay. He turned and headed out to sea.

The storm came full force out of the south. The semi shuddered as ten to twelve-meter waves rolled under the weather deck and periodically broke over the railings. The crew were all well aware that they were probably safe but must be ready for any problems or hazards that might develop. Few slept as the storm's fury looked for unwitting victims in the cold waters of the South Atlantic.

From the bridge of the semi the captain and first mate squinted as they tried to watch the dark sea around them through the driving rain. High-intensity lights were directed outward all around the platform, and they could see the fierce, foamy waves rolling continuously into the upright supports of the semi. Every seventh wave was a little bigger than the previous six, and these shook the platform with low grinding sounds that gave everyone a feeling of unease. Anchored about one kilometer north and south of the semi were two buoys that measured wave heights. These are called wave riders, and their information was telemetered constantly back to the bridge. The captain watched the digital readout of incoming data with growing concern.

"I think we're getting the occasional buildup, which could form a rogue," the captain informed the first mate.

The first mate pursed his lips. Both he and the captain were veterans of many seasons at sea in the South Atlantic. Their intuition told them this was going to be a bad night. There was nothing to be said, and nothing much to do except hold on and make sure the emergency crews were on their toes. They knew, however, that they didn't have to inform any of the crew as to the magnitude nor the dangers of this storm. Everyone was on standby.

Peek looked like a furtive gray drop of water in the huge dark rolling waves. The wave crests hissed ominously as wind caught water and whipped it into foam, forming long white streaks across the turbulent ocean. Now and then Peek was visible as he leapt above the wave crests into the driving rain to suck in air through his blowhole. Mountains of water ten meters high rose and fell as their peaks continued to spew the foamy mist off the sixty kilometers per hour winds. Peek dove deep to avoid the turbulence from the big waves. He surfaced every five or ten minutes and paced himself as he swam into the storm.

The 30,000-ton *Atlantic Stroom* rocked uncomfortably in the gale. A semi-submersible is much like an iceberg, with more than seventy percent of its ballast weight below water. But the towering fifty-meter drill derrick swayed like some kind of bizarre metronome to the rhythm of the storm.

Below deck the crew sat in the recreation lounges and talked in quiet voices. Some watched movies, but their minds were not on the entertainment. Mostly they listened to every creak and moan given up by the *Atlantic Stroom*. The crew knew every sound their vessel made, and one that didn't belong would be immediately recognized. Everyone's stomach was unsettled from the motion of the storm.

"How long do these last?" Madeleine asked. She was curled up on the small couch in Jonas's cabin. Mary Beth was next to her. Both women looked a little green from seasickness, as they hung on to the railing above the bunk.

"Could be days before this one blows itself out," Jonas said. He leaned away from gravity as the room swayed; it was a natural movement, and he subconsciously noted when the angle was excessive.

"I don't feel too good," Mary Beth said with a low moan. She had already dashed to the head and had come back clutching her belly. The room pitched suddenly, and her eyes grew wide with fear. She and Madeleine looked at Jonas.

"That was a big one." Jonas peered through the glass of the porthole, but there was nothing to see in the darkness. "So, Maddy, tell me about your class this year!" Jonas said, trying to get their minds off the storm. Madeleine rolled her eyes as if to say, *I just don't care about that right now*, and wrapped her arms around her waist.

"Captain," the first mate said in a steady voice. He kept his eyes fixed on the wave rider readout that the captain had been watching earlier.

"Hmmm. That's not good. Looks like the southern buoy has broken loose. There's another fifty thousand dollars down the drain."

"Yes sir, but look here, just before it went. It is huge . . ."

The captain glanced down briefly. He'd seen this before. He walked quickly to the south-facing window. The bridge was dark and lit only by subdued red lights from the compass, important engine room dials, stability control indicators, and the wave buoy charts. His squinting gaze under furrowed brow followed the beams of high-intensity spotlights that lit up the ocean around his vessel. He put his nose near the glass as if being that much closer to the storm would improve his vision. It mattered little. Through the driving rain he could still see the waves in the floodlights. As he watched, the sea seemed to drain back from the *Atlantic Stroom*, then the black water rose up hissing with foam. The captain's eyes grew wide, and he turned sharply to the first mate. "Sound the alarm!"

The first mate hammered his fist down onto a red button that triggered a blaring klaxon. Red emergency lights came on in every corridor, and the crew clamored for handholds.

"What's that!?" Madeleine yelled as she jumped to the sudden alarm.

"Something's wrong, must be a big wave," Jonas said. "Hang on tight!"

The rogue wave, the sum total of several different over-lapping waves lengths coalescing into one, rose up as a towering wall of water and slammed into the *Atlantic Stroom*. The impact sent the crew flying around their cabins and tumbling through the recreation room. Pots and pans in the galley crashed to the floor; books in the semi's library became airborne and scattered off the shelves. The wave crest towered seven meters above the weather deck—the total height was twenty-seven meters— eighty-one feet high! It broke over the deck and poured tons of water onto the drill platform. Metal groaned and creaked under the weight. Equipment and supplies tied down on deck were torn away and washed overboard. The vessel listed dangerously lee-ward as the mass of water within the wave passed through open decks. The crew could feel girders snapping and rivets popping as they clung to tables and counters behind watertight doors, their ears to cold metal. There was nothing anyone could do.

In less than ten seconds the wave was gone, but it had felt like an eternity. Jonas could feel the vessel struggling to right itself as the pontoons' ballast fought with the forces of nature. He held his breath as the *Atlantic Stroom* continued to pitch over, then paused and slowly edged itself back to upright like a stubborn dog. He let out a great sigh of relief and smiled at Madeleine and Mary Beth. Their faces were white with terror.

The captain, who had been tossed across the bridge like a rag doll, pulled himself to his feet and quickly began assessing dam-age. They were still afloat and his craft was righting itself—*it was a bloody good platform*, he thought to himself—and he thanked the stars and Neptune and God and everyone else he could think of for making it through that wave. There was, however, lots of damage. The crew began to report in from all over the *Atlantic Stroom:* ruptured side plates here, popped rivets there, torqued girders below deck, and several flooded compartments where the watertight doors had failed. Some of the crew were injured, but none were lost.

The first mate managed to get to his feet as well and began checking monitors and sensors that relayed the structural state of the ballast tanks and pontoons. What he saw was not good.

"Captain, we have serious problems on the starboard pontoon."

And there it was. Tensiometers, which monitored how much stress and strain existed on the *Atlantic Stroom*'s main supports and pontoons, were registering excessive damage below the waterline. That pontoon had been an ongoing problem, and the repairs that had been made, though strong, were not a match for the continued onslaught from the fierce energy of the ocean. The *Atlantic Stroom* would have to be towed to Cape Town for a complete refit if they survived this storm. But for the moment, the semi would surely sink if the forward main support on the starboard side was not repaired soon.

The captain reached for the phone and called Jonas Jeremy James.

CHAPTER

15

What you have seen, you know.
What you have not seen, you must believe.
Namibian proverb

The black hole looked particularly uninviting at the moment. Willy Drusbury and Piet Van Rooyen stood at Jonas's side. Jonas was suited up and seemed to be in a meditative mood.

"Well?" Piet said, more to himself than the others as he held on to one of the railings around the moon pool. The rise and fall of the water in the moon pool was mesmerizing—it had a dangerous frothy look to it, and the floodlights gave the water a turbid green appearance.

"Well, well," Jonas said. He too held on against the continuous rocking of the *Atlantic Stroom*. "I guess there's nothing keeping us from getting this job done, right, boys? Piet, is the Mutt ready? Willy, does the lifeline check out?"

The captain had reviewed the problems with Jonas, Willy, and Piet. They all knew only Jonas could do the job that needed to be done. The captain had silently put a hand on Jonas's shoulder after the briefing. His lips pressed tightly together in concern, he hoped Jonas, the most experienced diver he'd ever met, could save the *Atlantic Stroom*.

The problem was severe structural damage along the top of the forward starboard pontoon upon which was welded the support structure for the entire vessel. Jonas had told the captain he could only apply Bandaids so many times, that full refitting was really needed. The captain agreed and promised a visit to the shipyards as soon as the storm passed. The captain also knew it was all about budgets, prioritization, corporate goals, and playing the odds at sea. This time the dice had rolled against them.

Inside the hollow steel supports some of the crew were already working on reinforcing accessible parts of the pontoon, but much work needed to be done on the outside—underwater. The damage was approaching fatal for the *Atlantic Stroom*, but it would be immediate if another rogue wave struck, and the storm was far from over. Outside, fifteen-meter waves rolled under the deck and sent shudders throughout the riveted and welded skeleton of the steel island.

What Jonas was about to do was extremely dangerous. Before he left his cabin in the crew quarters Madeleine hugged him tight and said, "You can't go down there, you *know* what it's like outside! I didn't come all this way just to watch you drown. Tell the captain *no!* "

Jonas explained to her that if he didn't try to make the repair, then the entire platform would be imperiled. Then where would they all be? So he quickly hugged Madeleine and Mary Beth. "I love you, Maddy. This is my job, this is what I do," was all he could say. He quickly walked from the cabin and worked his way down to the black hole. The women were led by a crewman through the internal stairways to join Bebe in the weather station, where he was monitoring the storm. The view from this topside point was at once terrifying and fascinating as the storm embraced the *Atlantic Stroom*. Bebe watched the weather and wave data and the vessel's stability data, and he was in constant communication with the bridge. He also had a video link to the ROV so they could watch Jonas working.

As before, the welding torch and hoses were lowered down to the pontoon. The Mutt was deployed, and Piet maneuvered it down through the black hole and into the open ocean beneath the *Atlantic Stroom*. Immediately the currents and turbulence from the storm grabbed the Mutt and shook it.

"Not nice down there, Jonas," Piet said as he studied the video and constantly adjusted the motion of the ROV using the joysticks. He could see the wall of steel that was the starboard pontoon in the floodlights. Visibility was very poor, so he moved the Mutt quite close to the pontoon, now and then bumping it as furtive currents took control.

Jonas nodded. He could see the trouble Piet was having. "Yeah. It's gonna be a rough ride tonight."

"I want you to wear this air tank," Willy said, "just in case you lose control or anything happens to the cables. I want you to have a backup air supply."

"Not a bad idea, but it'll slow me down," Jonas said, but he didn't refuse the tank and slipped it over his shoulders. He clipped his safety line onto the Mutt's umbilical, then he clipped his own umbilical to his dive helmet and plugged it in. "Okay, then, wish me luck!" he said over the intercom.

The water grabbed him like a cold fist, and as the chill seeped into his wet suit it took his breath away. Soon, though, it was warmed by his body and the heated water pumped through his umbilical. He gave Piet and Willy a thumbs up and began his descent. As he swam down the black hole and into the murky ocean he could feel the tug and pull of chaotic turbulence from the fierce storm above. It was as if the ocean were furious at Jonas for venturing into its depths, and the waves tried to dig deep to get at him. But despite the storm's anger, he was securely clipped into the lines and soon joined the Mutt alongside the starboard pontoon.

"I can see stress cracks very clearly," Jonas said over the comlink. "This must be where the leaks are occurring." He continued his inspection along the pontoon. "Willy, it's a lot worse than we thought, there are stress cracks all along here, I'm going to have to do a lot of welding just to stabilize this section. Send down more steel, and I'll get to work."

"Roger that. We can see the damage on the video, and I'll inform the captain. Willy glanced at Piet who gave him a concerned look. The *Atlantic Stroom* shuddered in the storm, as if overhearing their conversation.

"We are in a bad way," Piet said in a low voice, as he continued to feel the waves pounding the *Atlantic Stroom*. This was a killer storm.

"How can he see what he's doing?" Mary Beth asked Bebe as she studied the video monitor. All she could see was the brilliant light of the welding torch, a chaotic mass of bubbles, and a vague human form.

"Jonas will be very focused on what he's welding and unaware of anything else. His field of view is very limited, especially with the welding visor down—all he can see is right where the flame is melting steel."

"Is he okay?" Madeleine asked. She hugged herself from worry as she watched her brother at work.

"Jonas is the best there is. Oh, he'll be good and tired after this one, but he will save this platform. Dead right," Bebe said and gave Madeleine a reassuring smile. But the smile hid considerable disquietude. The storm was intensifying, rather than abating, and the chance of another rogue wave was ever increasing. *Come on, dolphinman, fix this fragile boat.*

The tense hours slowly crept by.

Jonas shut down the torch and raised his welding visor. Under the floodlights he inspected his work. He felt fairly certain the worst of the damage had been repaired. With that realization the fatigue of the task, punctuated by the cold Atlantic waters, sank into his muscles, causing them to ache and shiver.

Suddenly his senses were shocked into alertness. He whirled around but could see only the yellowish-gray form of the Mutt in the murky water. The floodlights penetrated only a few meters.

"Got something," Piet said over the comlink.

"Yeah, me too," Jonas said, and at that moment a huge gray form passed in front of the floodlights. Jonas cowered back against the steel wall of the pontoon. The silhouette of the ragged jaws of Old Death sent a primal chill right through him.

"Looks like . . ." Piet began to say.

"Shark!" Jonas yelled into the microphone mounted in his face mask. The monster had already swam out of view.

"We're getting you up now, right now," Willy yelled. "Get over to the Mutt, and we'll pull everything up!"

"Yeah . . ." Jonas began to say, but he felt a tug. Then another stronger one, and he was pulled away from the pontoon. Old Death was gnawing at the life support cables. "I . . . It's chewing, Will . . ."

The comlink went dead.

"What's going on?" Piet yelled. "I'm not getting Jonas." He whirled the Mutt around and found the diver flailing in the murky water, hands to his face mask and kicking wildly. Piet could see the life support cable drift downward past Jonas. It had been severed. "That bloody shark has chewed through the cables!"

"He's drifting!" Willy yelled. "Follow him with the Mutt, grab him with that mechanical arm!"

Piet revved the ROV's small motors, and the Mutt took off after Jonas. In the video monitor they could see Jonas rip off his face mask and grope around for the spare tank's mouthpiece. He found it and jammed it in his mouth. He quickly put on his spare dive mask. A sudden flurry of bubbles told them that Jonas was breathing again, and they watched him adjust and clear his mask so he could again see.

Jonas immediately realized what Piet was trying to do and kicked hard against the current toward the Mutt. But in the monitor Willy and Piet saw the diver suddenly rear back as the massive form of the shark swam between him and the ROV.

Jonas kicked hard away from the shark. It was enormous, and it wagged back and forth as it circled him. Jonas could tell that Piet was driving the ROV toward him, but Old Death kept swimming between them—the shark knew what it wanted, and it wanted Jonas. It had already broken one tooth on the steel-armed Mutt. The current soon carried the Mutt and Jonas clear of the *Atlantic Stroom*. They were now in open ocean, and Jonas knew that Piet had only two kilometers of cable before the Mutt would be tethered like a dog at the end of its chain. Jonas had to do something fast, for in this current the length of cable would be used up quickly.

Old Death lived by one rule—survival of the fittest. He was willing to test the fitness of any animal in the ocean. He particularly hated humans, because of the hunting they had done from their boats. Old Death had taken many divers and knew their ways well. This one had evaded him once; he would not again.

Old Death circled one more time and then lunged toward his prey.

Jonas barely had time to react. In the glow from the flashlights strapped to his arm and headgear, he saw the jagged maw of the shark open toward him as the white lids closed over its eyes. Jonas kicked once hard, then balled up as he spun around. The shark collided with the air tank on Jonas's back and bit down hard on the steel. Jonas sucked in one last breath and released the catches on the harness. Old Death shook the tank back and forth as he tried to tear the object to pieces. Jonas shot up toward the surface for air and life—well aware that he only had moments before the cruel effects of rapid decompression would overtake him. He had no choice.

Piet and Willy watched in horror at the sudden change of events. From the weather room Madeleine screamed as she watched the video monitor and saw the shark lunge toward her brother. But then Jonas was free and swimming upward. Piet steered the ROV to follow Jonas's ascent. He hoped beyond hope that he would at least be able to recover Jonas when he succumbed to the bends. Old Death realized the folly of devouring an air tank and gave chase to the ascending diver.

Jonas felt his lungs would explode as he broke through to the surface. Gulping air and seawater, he looked up at a towering fifteen-meter wave as it broke over his head. Gulping air again, he dove quickly under it and struggled back to the surface. The storm tossed him about like sea foam, and the horizontal rain stung his face. His joints began to ache—the first sign of the bends. But then the massive dark form of Old Death appeared on the surface, its dorsal fin slicing the turbulent water like a relentless saber.

Suddenly Jonas felt a nudge under his arm. He spun around and there was Peek!

"Swim!" Peek commanded. "Swim and hang on to my fin."

Old Death, sensing the dolphin, rolled and dove in fury as he swam toward the diver. *I will eat them both . . .*

The ROV reached the surface and rolled violently in the waves, its lamps shining erratically here and there in the storm. But the whole scene was bathed in the rain-filtered floodlights of the *Atlantic Stroom*. From the bridge the captain and first mate alternated between watching through the window and glancing at the ROV's video monitor.

Bebe could just make out the drama through the rainpelted window of the weather station. Madeleine and Mary Beth were glued to the chaotic images on the video monitor as the ROV was tossed about in the waves, now and then stabilized enough by Piet that they could see the shark, Jonas, and the dolphin. Bebe said to Madeleine, "Stay here!" and he flung open the outer door, going to the deck railing in the face of the storm. He grabbed the lever for one of the semi's spotlights and directed it onto the water. He tried to focus it on Jonas, but everything was moving, and the rain burned like bee stings. Lightning flashed like a strobe light, imparting a bizarre vision of the turmoil at hand.

Jonas's sister could not sit still. Madeleine and Mary Beth were at Bebe's side in the driving rain, searching the foamy water. Despair rose in all of them: *How could any person live through this?*

Bebe spotted an enormous fin among the waves. It was the shark. "There!" he bellowed into the wind. Then, following the direction of the shark, he spotted Jonas. "By the sands of the Namib! Your brother is holding on to that dolphin!"

Madeleine and Mary Beth cheered in new hope.

Jonas was having serious trouble. He had swallowed a lot of water, and the sudden decompression was taking its toll on his system. Muscles and joints cramped up, and he gritted his teeth against the pain. *I'm dying. I'm dying.*

"Jonas, you must swim like me, not just with me. Concentrate on me. Swim. Pump your legs as I do my flukes. Concentrate, Jonas, it is the only way." Peek could sense Old Death very near. The big old shark was strong and fast and unwavering, its mind set. Peek was the fastest thing in the ocean. But he was using all of his strength and determination to pull Jonas along at ever increasing speeds.

Jonas focused on Peek. He clung to the dolphin and pumped his legs as Peek had told him. He, too, could sense Old Death so near, so threatening, and he pumped harder. Peek and Jonas gulped air in unison and dove. The shark was close behind, and the two came up again.

From the weather station railing Bebe, Madeleine, and Mary Beth followed the drama with the spotlight. They gasped as they saw the great white shark closing rapidly on Jonas and the dolphin. Dagger teeth glistened momentarily in the wavering lights. They watched as the man and dolphin dove, surfaced, and dove again in unison.

Madeleine was breathless as she wiped both tears and rain from her eyes to see the dance-like beauty of the dolphin and her brother swimming together. *How is he doing this? How is this possible?* she asked herself.

Piet lost control of the Mutt as a wave tore at it and tossed it wildly into the frothing ocean. He looked at Willy, and they both ran to the upper decks and joined Bebe and the others at the weather station railing.

In the turbulence the chase continued. Peek had dodged the shark and turned, bringing Jonas back toward the *Atlantic Stroom*. Jonas looked up at the massive steel island and could see the line of people at the railing, watching the life-and-death scene. He felt himself dive and then leap clear of the water into the driving rain next to Peek. Now his hand just barely clung to the dolphin's dorsal fin. He gulped air again and dove with Peek.

"There!" cried Madeleine. And she pointed to her brother and the dolphin leaping high to flee from the great white shark.

"Concentrate, Jonas," Peek said. "It is the only way. Concentrate." Peek urged his friend on. They were outdistancing Old Death. Peek and Jonas leapt from the sea again.

Bebe saw the dolphin and Jonas leap from the turbulent sea and again dive beneath the waves. *If that dolphin can just get Jonas back to the wash deck*, he said to himself. He watched them in awe as they leapt and dove in their attempt to evade the shark.

Jonas leapt from the sea again and could see Peek next to him, but he did not have to hold onto his friend.

From the guard rail of the weather station Bebe, Madeleine, Mary Beth, Willy, and Piet saw Jonas and the dolphin again dive beneath the waves. The great white shark surged out of the water and followed them into the foaming mix. And then only two dolphins emerged—leaping high and free from the shark. One of the dolphins spun majestically in the stormy air before they both vanished into the next wave.

Chapter

16

A good friend is like a brother.
Namibian proverb

Madeleine sat at the window of the helicopter. Tears misted her eyes. She waved farewell to Bebe. As he waved back, she placed one hand over her mouth to hold back the sorrow of her loss, her other hand clinging tightly to Mary Beth's.

The sea was calm now. It gave no hint of its former fury, no inkling of regret in the events that had transpired. Madeleine now understood the ocean as a living organism, how it was alive with life and energy. She placed a hand on the window of the helicopter as she looked out over the expanse of blue.

The helicopter lifted off from the deck, turned into the wind, and flew low over the placid water. It had taken two more days before the storm had blown itself out. The repairs Jonas had performed had saved the *Atlantic Stroom*. His body was never recovered, and they had held an honorary burial at sea for him under the clear skies that followed the storm. He was missed by the entire crew.

Now, as Madeleine looked out the window, she saw what looked like a moving coral reef with perpetual breakers. She realized it was the dolphins. They leapt and hurtled themselves through the air like convex torpedos with rainbow trails, swift and glistening. She felt a sudden rush of emotion and again placed her hand on the window as she watched the magic and fluid forms. There were nearly a thousand dolphins. Two large ones were in the lead. As the helicopter passed them, one leapt impossibly high out of the water and spiraled majestically in the air.

For a brief instant its eye locked with her own, and she knew where Jonas had gone.

To find a true friend is to find the answer.
Namibian proverb

Madeleine had entrusted to Bebe the huge diamond Jonas had given her. Months later, back in Mystic, the tall Namibian showed up at her door with a huge smile on his face. He had gone to Antwerp, to the Diamantkwartier—the diamond quarter—and sold the diamond for a fortune. All of the money came to Madeleine. Overwhelmed at this turn of events, she ask Bebe to emigrate to the United States and help her manage the Jonas Dolphin Research Fund at the local aquarium.

Once a year, Bebe, Madeleine, and Mary Beth travel down to Cape Town. There they charter a helicopter and fly along the coast with the hope of catching a glimpse of the dolphins.

But that's another story.

ABOUT THE AUTHOR

Roger Kuhns holds a PhD in geology. He has worked for 35 years around the world in over 80 countries and in the South Atlantic. He has taught at City College of New York and University of Wisconsin Field Station. Roger also teaches geology and writing at The Clearing in Ellison Bay, Wisconsin. He writes and performs monologues about his life, and has written and produced two films. He finds adventure in every corner of the globe, and every corner of his life. Roger lives in Mystic, Connecticut, with his wife, Anne, and their two cats.

You can follow Roger at:
www.rogerjameskuhns.com

He invites readers to e-mail him at:
rogerjameskuhns@gmail.com

Also available as an eBook

www.ingramcontent.com/pod-product-compliance
Lightning Source LLC
Chambersburg PA
CBHW060619310726
48982CB00003B/612